Now Picture This

ROBIN JONES GUNN

BETHANY HOUSE PUBLISHERS

MINNEAPOLIS, MINNESOTA 55438

Now Picture This
Copyright © 1998, Robin Jones Gunn

Edited by Janet Kobobel Grant
Cover design by Praco, Ltd. Cover illustration by George Angelini

Sierra's response to the hot-line caller in chapter 8 was contributed by Angela Dixon, the winner of the 1997 Sierra Jensen/*Brio* writing contest on the topic of purity.

Scripture quotations taken from *New American Standard Bible* © 1960, 1977 by the Lockman Foundation; and *The Holy Bible, New International Version* © 1973, 1984 by International Bible Society, used by permission of Zondervan Publishing House. All rights reserved.

A Focus on the Family book published by
Bethany House Publishers
A Ministry of Bethany Fellowship International
11300 Hampshire Avenue South, Minneapolis, Minnesota 55438
www.bethanyhouse.com

Printed in the United States of America by
Bethany Press International, Minneapolis, Minnesota 55438

Library of Congress Cataloging-in-Publication Data

Gunn, Robin Jones, 1955–
    Now picture this / Robin Jones Gunn.
       p.   cm. — (The Sierra Jensen series ; 9)
    Summary: While spending all of her time corresponding with and daydreaming about her friend Paul, who attends college in Scotland, Sierra Jensen finds the real world around her falling apart.
    ISBN 1–56179–636–0
    [1. Interpersonal relations—Fiction. 2. Christian life—Fiction.]
I. Title. II. Series: Gunn, Robin Jones, 1955–   Sierra Jensen series ; 9.
PZ7.G972No   1998
[Fic]—DC21   98–21107
                                        CIP
                                        AC

98 99 00 01 02 03 04 05 / 15 14 13 12 11 10 9 8 7 6 5 4 3 2 1

To Amanda Joy Johnson

May your life continue to shine, my dear niece.

chapter one

"**S**OMEBODY ANSWER THE DOORBELL," SIERRA'S MOM called from the kitchen.

Sierra paused at the top of the stairs with an envelope in her hand. She had just arrived home from school and had found the eagerly awaited letter from Paul. Wanting to hide in her bedroom and soak up every word, she had taken the stairs two at a time. But she found her room invaded by Uncle Matthew; his wife, Abby; and their three young boys. The Jensen household was expecting a record-setting 31 family members for Thanksgiving dinner tomorrow.

"Howard, can you answer the door?" Mrs. Jensen called to her husband, since no one had responded to her first plea.

Sierra wedged her slim frame into the corner alcove at the top of the stairs, out of view from the entryway, and carefully opened the envelope postmarked "Edinburgh." She unfolded the onionskin paper. Paul had written with bold, black letters at the top of the letter:

When it rains it seems the world
Takes on a somber hue
My soul is hushed
I lift my pen
And write a song for You.

Sierra drew in a quick breath and read Paul's poem one more time. Closing her eyes, lost in a dream, she tilted her head back and hit the wall a little too hard. The glass globe on the wall's antique light fixture tilted off its perch and tumbled to the floor before Sierra realized what had happened. It hit the rug with a dull thump and split in two. Sierra carefully picked up the pieces and tried to fit them back into the light fixture's base. But the pieces wouldn't stay in place.

Downstairs the voices of Aunt Emma, Uncle Jack, and their twin daughters, Amanda and Kayla, filled the entryway. Howard Jensen's booming "Hello! Come in, come in!" welcomed them.

Above the rush of excited voices, Sierra's mom called from the kitchen, "Sierra, I need a hand in here."

"Coming." Sierra quickly folded the letter into the envelope and tucked it in the front pouch pocket of her sweatshirt. *I'll be back*, she silently vowed to the letter, giving it a pat. *Just as soon as I can.*

Then, taking the broken globe with her, Sierra hurried downstairs to greet her relatives. She handed her dad the two pieces of glass. "Upstairs, first light on the right. Sorry. I bumped the wall."

"Put it over there on the entry table." Worry lines

creased Howard Jensen's forehead. "I'll see to it after I get the door back on the china cabinet."

Sierra followed the caravan of company into the kitchen. Sierra's mother, in the thick of her pumpkin pie preparations, greeted them, promising hugs as soon as she placed the pies in the oven.

"Sierra, open the oven door for me, will you?" her mom asked. She was trying to sound nice even though Sierra knew she was frazzled.

"You were supposed to wait and let us help you with that, Sharon." Emma stepped over and brushed a kiss across Sierra's mom's cheek. "Thanks for doing all this and putting up with the craziness. It means a lot to have so many family members together again."

"We're glad everyone could make it," Sharon Jensen said graciously. "It'll be fun."

Sierra suppressed a grin at the word "fun." She knew this kind of pressure was not her mom's idea of a great time.

"Where's Granna Mae?" Emma asked about Sierra's grandmother.

"Upstairs, I think." Sierra's mom carefully balanced a pumpkin pie in each hand as Sierra held open the wobbly oven door. She knew if she let go of the door that it would tilt to the side. Her dad had worked on it last week, but it was crooked again and needed to be held steady.

Sierra was about to close the mouth of the ancient dragon oven when her mom said, "Wait. Two more pies."

"Sierra," her dad called over his shoulder, "I'm going

to set up Jack and Emma here in the study. Could you run upstairs and let Granna Mae know they're here?"

The last thing Sierra wanted was to start running errands for everyone. She had a letter waiting for her. A wonderful, romantic letter warming her pocket.

"Wait a second," her mom said. "Before you run upstairs, Sierra, could you check on the boys for me? I think they're still in the backyard, but I haven't heard or seen them for the past half-hour. And don't let Brutus in the house."

Sierra sighed and reluctantly headed for the back door. A swirl of huge, amber-colored leaves had collected in front of the doorway. They were sent flying down the stairs and back into the yard when she opened the screen door.

"Dillon! Gavin!" Sierra called. "Where are you guys?"

The only response was the bellowing "Woof!" of Brutus, their lovable "lug of a fur ball," as Sierra's older brother Wesley called the dog. Sierra was glad Wes was coming home from college for Thanksgiving. This was his senior year, and even though Corvallis was only two hours away, Wes had hardly been home all fall. Of Sierra's four brothers, she was closest to Wesley. Something inside her suspected he had a girlfriend. He had told their dad that he might bring a guest home with him, but Mr. Jensen hadn't thought to ask if the guest was male or female.

Wes had volunteered to pick up Tawni, Sierra's only sister, at the airport on his way home. The two of them and the possible mysterious guest were expected to arrive after nine that night.

"Sorry, Brutus," Sierra said, stuffing her chilled hands into the pouch pocket of her sweatshirt. The letter warmed her fingers when she touched it. "You can't come in for the next few days, buddy. Get used to that doghouse."

The chain on his collar kept Brutus from venturing beyond the lawn's edge. He barked loudly, as if complaining about his confinement.

"I know. It's rough on all of us, Brutus. You should see where I have to sleep. Tawni and I get the floor in Granna Mae's room, along with Nicole, Aunt Frieda, and Molly. It's a tight squeeze. And Dad says Aunt Frieda snores."

Brutus responded with what Sierra supposed was a sympathetic bark. A shiver ran through her. She could feel the chilling raindrops hit her long, blonde hair. Oregon's moisture made her hair curlier than it was naturally, which frustrated her. Only the weight of her hair kept her from being a total fuzzhead.

Most of her friends had long, sleek hair, but they were continually telling Sierra they loved her wild, free-flowing curls, which matched her personality. Sierra would trade hair with any of them.

She pulled the hood of her oversized sweatshirt over her head. "You'd better stay out of the wet, Brutus. Where are Gavin and Dillon; do you know?"

Then she noticed that the light was on in her dad's workshop. The small structure was originally a playhouse complete with shutters and gingerbread trim along the roof. But Howard Jensen had turned it into a haven for his power tools and workbench.

A person approaching the dollhouse would expect to find little girls in big hats playing tea party at a small, lace-covered table, but instead the doors opened to a pint-sized hardware store with pegboard walls and fluorescent over-head lighting.

Sierra pushed Brutus away with her leg before he could jump up on her as she sprinted through the rain.

She approached the workshop and called out, "Dillon, Gavin, are you guys in here?"

Opening the door, she found her two elementary-school-age brothers busily moving equipment around in the tight quarters. A stack of blankets was on the work-bench.

"What are you guys doing? Didn't you hear me calling you?"

"We're going to sleep out here."

"Says who?" Sierra asked, her hand automatically snap-ping to her hip as she took on her motherly voice.

"We don't want to sleep in Mom and Dad's room with those other boys."

"You mean Jared, Bob, and Marshall? They're your cousins. What's wrong with them? You guys are all about the same age. You'll have a good time."

Dillon and Gavin looked at each other skeptically.

Sierra realized the five young boy cousins hadn't been around each other since they were babies. They didn't have a relationship even though they were related. Sierra knew what that was like. She had felt the same way toward Nicole and Molly five years ago, when they had been together for Christmas. The three preteen cousins had a rocky beginning with a misunderstanding over who would sleep in which bed, but they had ended up friends before the holiday was over. And that time they all had beds to sleep in, not an allotted corner of floor space like this year. Sierra understood how her brothers could feel outnumbered by three boys they didn't know and yet were expected to treat nicely.

"Why don't you guys wait until after you've spent some time with them? You might like them. Besides, it's going to get cold out here."

"We don't care. We brought all the blankets."

"Yeah, and I'm sure Mom's not going to be crazy about that. She'll need blankets for all the people sleeping in the house. Come on. Let's go in. Mom and Dad are counting on us to be hospitable."

"What's that mean?" Gavin asked.

"It means you be nice. Come on. And bring the blankets with you."

Sierra opened the door and motioned for the boys to dash through the rain back into the house. They took their time, lugging the blankets and looking like refugees leaving their homeland.

"Come on," Sierra said, jogging ahead of them to get out of the persistent rain. "You're getting the blankets wet."

Brutus emerged from his doghouse and bounded out to meet them.

"Back!" Sierra yelled. "Don't even think about jumping on us. You stay in your house."

"Yeah," Gavin echoed. "Be a-spittable, Brutus. At least you get your own bed tonight."

Sierra opened the back door, kicking away the now soggy yellow leaves and calling to her brothers to hurry up. When they entered the warm, fragrant kitchen, and Mrs. Jensen saw the stack of blankets, her eyes grew huge.

"What are you doing? Did those get wet? Sierra, why didn't you stop them?"

"I . . . they . . ."

Mrs. Jensen ran a hand over the top blanket and snapped at Sierra, "Take these down to the basement and put them in the dryer on low. Make sure it's low, or these wool ones will be ruined. Don't put more than two in at a time. You boys get cleaned up. I don't want you going outside anymore. It's too wet."

Sierra briskly grabbed the blankets from her brothers and tromped down to the cold, musty basement, muttering all the way, " 'Get the boys, Sierra-ella.' 'Check on your grandmother, Sierra-ella.' 'Stoke the fire, wash the floors, scrub the hearth, pluck the chicken, mend the . . .' "

Before she could continue her exaggerated chore list, Sierra noticed her dad coming up the basement stairs with a plunger in his hand. Their old house often had plumbing problems.

"The upstairs bathroom is already clogged." He looked as stressed as his wife, and his jaw was set as if to say "Get outta my way."

Sierra flattened herself and the bundle of blankets against the wall as her dad marched past her. Apparently, she wasn't the only one who was suffering from a Cinderella complex this holiday.

As he passed by, Sierra's dad's concretely set jaw opened only wide enough for him to mutter, "This is going to be a long weekend."

chapter two

ALL SIERRA WANTED TO DO WAS TO FIND A QUIET place to hide so she could read Paul's letter. But as soon as the first round of blankets was in the dryer, she still needed to check on Granna Mae. She loved her dear, though often confused, grandma. The letter would have to wait a few more minutes while Sierra flew up the stairs to check on Granna Mae.

If the rest of us are this stressed, she wondered, *how is Granna Mae handling all the activity?*

This large Victorian house was actually Granna Mae's; she had lived here her entire married life, and her nine children had grown up here. Sierra's father was the oldest, and Emma was the youngest. The second oldest son, Paul, had died in Vietnam. The rest were still alive, and three of them—Frieda, Matthew, and Emma—were coming with their families for the Thanksgiving weekend.

Almost a year ago, Sierra's family had moved in with Granna Mae because she could no longer live on her own. Her condition varied; some days she was bright as a berry, but other days she needed to be watched constantly so she wouldn't wander off in a daze.

Sierra knocked softly on Granna Mae's bedroom door. When Sierra didn't hear a reply, she called out, "Granna Mae, may I come in?"

She pushed the door open and peeked inside. Granna Mae was asleep in her cozy recliner by the window with the radio softly playing classical music. Sierra tiptoed past the bed mats lining the floor, and reaching for a quilt from the end of Granna Mae's bed, she slipped it over the sleeping woman.

Outside, the rain pelted the windows. Sierra pulled down the shades and closed the heavy curtains to quiet the room and buffer the chill from the original 1915 windows. She stepped away, intending to leave the room, but then she stopped. Her pile of clothes and other belongings she would need for the weekend were stacked against the wall by the dresser, next to her bed mat. Her mom had insisted that Sierra and her little brothers clean their rooms exceptionally well and then take the things they needed over the weekend to the room where they would be sleeping so they wouldn't disturb the guests who had claimed their rooms.

In the middle of Sierra's stack on the floor was her favorite birthday gift. She tiptoed over to draw it out of the clothes. The instant her fingers touched the cool metal frame, Sierra smiled. She pulled out the picture and held it close in the dimness of the quiet bedroom. Soft violin and cello music floated from the radio as she took in the picture's image: Paul.

The framed photo showed Paul standing in hiking gear deep in the Scottish Highlands, with the wind whipping his dark hair across his forehead and giving his cheeks a ruddy glow. Apparently, he had been talking when he turned to face the camera because he looked as if he had just burst out laughing. Sierra focused on his eyes. One eyebrow was up slightly, and his blue-gray eyes almost shimmered, as if they caught the reflection off some pristine lake below him.

From where he stood on top of a rocky crag, the view behind him went on forever. And what a hopelessly romantic view it was: bright blue skies and velvet green hills dotted by windswept clumps of rose-tinted heather.

To Sierra, this wasn't just a picture. It wasn't merely a photograph. What she held in her hands was a window. A window framed in shiny brass. A window that allowed her to look out of her little corner of the world to see the view from Paul's life.

Since June, when Paul had gone to Scotland to stay with his recently widowed grandmother and to attend school in Edinburgh, Sierra had wondered what his world was like. She had prayed for this unique guy ever since their chance meeting at Heathrow Airport in London last January.

When Sierra's sister, Tawni, moved to Southern California and began to date Paul's brother, Jeremy, Paul's and Sierra's lives intersected again. Then, when she was given an assignment from her Christian high school to help out at the Highland House, she discovered that Paul's uncle

Mac ran the homeless shelter. Paul even worked there at the same time Sierra did.

Yet, despite all the bizarre coincidences and connections, Paul showed no special interest in Sierra. He had embarrassed her one night at Carla's Café, a charming coffeehouse in downtown Portland, when he had asked if she had a crush on him.

Sierra's answer apparently surprised Paul. She had stated that she wondered if maybe God brought people into others' lives at different times for specific reasons. She told Paul she thought they had met so she could pray for him, since, practically against her will, she had been prompted innumerable times to do just that.

Much seemed to have changed inside Paul during the first few months he was in Scotland. By the end of the summer, he had contacted Sierra and asked her to correspond with him. He suggested they write via "snail-mail," instead of e-mail, which she preferred, since he wanted their words to take their time traveling back and forth and not to be shot instantly from one end of the world to the other.

For weeks now they had been corresponding. Sierra wrote to Paul nearly every day, even if it was just a postcard or a few lines on a piece of notebook paper in class. And Paul wrote to her often. His words brought descriptions of the classes he attended, the people he spent time with, the funny things his grandmother said, and the way the autumn sun looked against the windowpane of his grandmother's cottage right before it slid behind the hills. Paul also wrote about what was on his heart—his feelings, his prayers, his quiet thoughts. He shared openly with Sierra, and she did the same.

All along she had had only words to aid her in looking into Paul MacKenzie's life. Now she had a window in her hand. Through this brass-framed window she saw more than the hills, the heather, and the brown leather jacket Paul had worn when they first met. She could now see the face, the eyes, and the smile of the guy who had turned her emotions inside out. No one had ever done that to her before—not like this.

Sierra felt a smile pull up the corners of her mouth as she ran her fingers across the clear glass of her picture, her window. She remembered how her fingers had trembled when her mom handed her the package from Paul on the day before her birthday. Sierra had ripped open the padded mailing envelope right there in the kitchen while her mom and her little brother Gavin watched. The gift came wrapped simply, in tan-flecked tissue tied with thin jute cord. Sierra remembered carefully pulling off the jute, thinking she could use it to macramé something—a bracelet, maybe. The tiny attached card said, "Happy Birthday, Daffodil Queen," which was Paul's nickname for her.

When she pulled out the picture, Gavin said, "That's all you got? Just a picture?"

Sierra wanted to cry when she looked at Paul's handsome face. If her mother and Gavin hadn't been there, she most certainly would have kissed the glass.

Now, in the stillness of Granna Mae's room, while the echo of another round of voices filled the entryway and circled up the stairs, Sierra pressed her lips to her index finger and touched Paul's wind-burned cheek with her finger. She knew she still had his unread words waiting for her in her pocket.

Balancing his picture on her crossed legs, Sierra reached for the letter and adjusted her position so she could get as much light as possible from the one low-lit lamp on Granna Mae's nightstand.

She unfolded the paper and read, her lips moving silently:

> *When it rains it seems the world*
> *Takes on a somber hue*
> *My soul is hushed*
> *I lift my pen*
> *And write a song for You.*

> *Sierra, my friend, it's a rainy night here. Can you tell? I'm at my grandmother's. I read your last letter on the train on the way home from school for the weekend, and I must confess I read every word twice. All three pages.*

> *I think what you said about your sister is true. It was good for her to write that letter to her birth mother, even though she hasn't heard back from her—even if she never does.*

> *Jeremy e-mailed me last week that he thinks Tawni is going to go back to school. Has she told you yet? He's been encouraging her to start with some night classes at the community college. I thought about you and all your big decisions about college next year. I remember what it was like having to send off all those applications before*

November 1 during my senior year. I'm glad you found out about the scholarship application and sent it in time. I imagine you'll have no trouble landing any scholarship you apply for. I hadn't realized you were a 4.0 girl. I should have guessed. You always do seem to have an answer for everything.

A sudden knock on the door made Sierra jump. Before she could stuff Paul's picture back in her stack of clothes or tuck away the letter, the door opened and her oldest brother, Cody, stepped in with his wife, Katrina, and their irrepressible toddler, Tyler.

"There's Auntie Sara," Cody said, using Tyler's nickname for Sierra as he released Tyler's hand so he could run over to Sierra where she sat cross-legged on the floor.

Sierra shot a cautious glance over at Granna Mae sleeping in the recliner. Cody followed her eyes and quickly apologized.

"Sorry," he said softly. "I didn't realize Granna Mae was napping."

Before Sierra could move, Tyler pounced on her. The heel of his little hiking boot crashed into the glass in Paul's picture.

"Tyler!" Sierra yelled.

He pulled back, startled by her response. The bend in his leg caught the corner of Paul's letter and tore the onionskin paper in two.

"Tyler!" she yelled again.

"Sierra," Katrina said with a definite scold in her voice.

Sierra grabbed the pieces of the letter and stuffed them

into her pocket. With the other hand, she quickly reached for Tyler's curious fingers as they were going for the shards of broken glass. "Don't touch. It will cut you."

"What's going on?" Granna Mae asked, blinking and pulling the blanket off her lap.

"It's okay," Cody said, going over to his grandmother and giving her a hug.

Katrina scooped Tyler off of Sierra's lap just as the startled and confused boy burst into tears. Without a word, Katrina headed for the bedroom door. Sierra knew her sister-in-law was mad.

"I'm sorry," Sierra said to her retreating back.

Tyler squirmed in his mom's arms, trying to get down. "Auntie Sara!" he cried. "I want Auntie Sara!"

Carrying her wailing son, Katrina left the room and closed the door behind her. Sierra heard Tyler's cries fading down the hallway. Cody, meanwhile, was trying to settle Granna Mae back down in her chair. In a soothing voice, he told her what was going on.

Sierra could still feel her heart pounding. How could so much have gone wrong so fast? Blinking to keep back the tears, she looked at the broken glass frame still balanced on her leg. At least the glass hadn't sliced into the photo or through her jeans, or so she hoped.

Rising and walking to the trash can by the door, Sierra let the broken pieces slip into the trash. She lifted the picture and examined it more closely. A tiny shard of glass still stuck in the photo. She tapped the back of the frame over the trash, dislodging the sharp fragment. Checking the photo again, she bit her lower lip when she realized the shard had left a mark. It was a tiny cut over Paul's heart.

chapter three

"**H**E DIDN'T MEAN TO DO IT," KATRINA SAID firmly to Sierra.

The two of them stood in the back corner of the kitchen while the rest of the group went through Mrs. Jensen's "chow line" and scooped their own bowls of soup from three large pots she had simmering on the stove. Everyone had arrived except Wesley and Tawni. The noise level in the tiny kitchen was unbearable. This many people had been at Sierra's birthday party the weekend before, but the noise hadn't irritated her the way this laughter and chattering did.

"I know," Sierra said. "He startled me, that's all. I didn't want him to get cut on the glass."

"I appreciate that," Katrina replied. "I'll be glad to replace whatever was broken. Was it a picture frame?"

Sierra nodded. "Don't worry. It's okay. The frame is fine. I can buy glass for it."

She smiled. Katrina smiled back.

"Where's Tyler now?" Sierra asked.

"He fell asleep on Gavin's bed. He didn't sleep in the

car on the way here as I hoped he would, so he crashed as soon as he stopped crying."

"I'd better check on him," Sierra said. "He might be frightened when he wakes up, if he doesn't know where he is."

Katrina nodded. "Thanks, Sierra. Do you want me to bring some soup up for you?"

"No, but you might want to see if anyone is taking some up for Granna Mae. I'm afraid we've rattled her, and Dad thought it would be better if she ate in her room rather than come down for dinner."

"I'll check on her," Katrina said.

Sierra smiled as she slid past the swarm of relatives and retreated to the quieter upstairs. She stopped by the hall closet to grab a flashlight off the upper shelf. When she was little, she thought this was a magical closet that led directly to Narnia. Tonight she would have welcomed a journey into that fictional world. A cup of tea with Mrs. Beaver would have been a treat.

Tyler was sound asleep on Gavin's bed, so Sierra positioned herself snugly in the beanbag chair in the corner. She kept the flashlight low and pulled the torn letter from her pocket, determined to read the entire missive before the evening was over. Scanning the sentences until she caught up to where she had left off, she read:

> . . . You always do seem to have an answer for every-
> thing. I mean that in a good way. You know what you
> want and what your life is all about. I wish I'd had that
> much clarity when I was your age. I guess God just

allowed me to take a little more of a winding trail to get to that point. But here I am. And I can honestly say I've never felt this much peace or this close to God. It's a good thing. Or what is it you said your friends say? It's a "God-thing"? Yes, it's definitely a God-thing.

My grandmother has insisted we ration the heating fuel this fall. I told you her cottage is old—make that ancient. When it's cold and wet here, it's really cold and wet. I have turned into a man of many layers. Even sitting around the house, I wear at least three layers with a wool sweater on top. I tried wearing my down jacket to dinner tonight, but Grandma said I was being rude and hit me with a wooden cooking spoon. (It didn't hurt a bit—couldn't feel a thing through all the layers!)

So as I write this in my "thrifty Scotch" bedroom, I'm wearing my down jacket and am wrapped in a wool blanket. Don't tell Granny, but I pinched one of her wee candles, and I have it lit here on the writing desk to thaw out my fingers between paragraphs. . . .

Ah, there; warm again. Now, what was I saying? It's a dark and stormy night here. The raindrops fling themselves at my window like desperadoes shouting, "Let us in! It has to be warmer in there than it is out here!" Ha! Little do the raindrops know it's the same temperature in here as it is out there. And in here one must deal with "the Grandmother." Out there all they have to deal with is the wind. Hmm . . . I'm thinking I might join them.

May the peace of Christ be upon you, dear Sierra.

Paul

Sierra drew in a deep breath and turned off the

flashlight. She always felt the same when she finished reading one of Paul's letters: wonderfully warmed and terribly disappointed. She felt disappointed that his words had stopped and the little bit of him she had in her hands had come to an end. And she felt warm on the inside. She wondered if Paul felt the same way when he read her letters.

Quietly lifting the shade on the window behind her, Sierra peeked out at the rainy world. The raindrops were just as Paul had described them: desperadoes beating against the glass. It made her wonder if Paul had any idea he was such a wonderful poet. She decided to tell him that in her next letter, a letter she would begin to write now.

With soft steps, she made her way over to Dillon's desk and reached for a pen and a blank piece of paper in the drawer. Returning to the beanbag chair with a book for a lap table, she balanced the flashlight on the windowsill so it shone away from the peacefully sleeping Tyler. Sierra began her letter.

Dear Poet,
You are, you know. I loved your "When It Rains" poem. Your timing is perfect because it's raining here, too. And I'm also thinking of you. Downstairs about a gazillion relatives have congregated so we can all be together for Thanksgiving tomorrow. But I've found a quiet spot beside a window where the desperado raindrops are now begging me to let them in. The funniest thing is that none of them sounds like a western desperado. They all have Scottish accents! Did you send them here to harass me? And if so, why didn't you come along with them? I would have let you in, and I can

guarantee it's warmer inside here than it is outside on this dark and stormy night.

She continued to write as Tyler slept. She filled four pages before the bedroom door opened. The light from the hallway flooded the room, and someone flipped on the bedroom light. Sierra squinted, trying to see who it was. Tyler woke up and immediately started to cry.

"Oh, I'm sorry," Caleb, her 14-year-old cousin, said. "My mom told me to bring my stuff up 'cuz I'm sleeping here. Why's he crying?" Caleb dropped his gear on the floor and cracked his knuckles nervously.

"It's okay," Sierra said, going to Tyler's side to comfort him. The minute she touched him she said, "Oh, baby, you're burning up."

She put her hand on his moist forehead. Tyler only cried louder.

"Caleb, tell Aunt Katrina to come up right away."

Caleb fled the room.

"You want a drink of water, Tyler?"

"I want my mommy!"

"She's coming, Little Bear. Here, let's take off this sweatshirt."

Tyler squirmed and resisted, but Sierra kept at it, knowing he would feel better.

"There. Now let me take off your socks. We have to cool you down."

Just then Katrina flew in the open door. She took over immediately, calmly asking Sierra to bring a cold washcloth and to find the liquid Tylenol in Katrina's cosmetic bag in the bathroom. By the time Sierra returned, Tyler had stopped crying and was sucking on his first two fingers as Katrina rocked him in her lap. After Sierra did all she could to help, she gathered up her papers and told Katrina she would slip out now.

"Homework?" Katrina asked, eyeing the many pages.

"Oh, no," Sierra said, feeling herself blush. "Just a letter."

"Oh?" Katrina responded, with a knowing smile. "You'll have to tell me about him sometime."

Sierra nodded and left. She hadn't told many people about Paul and their growing relationship. She had e-mailed Christy several times and had asked advice once or twice. And she had told her best friend, Vicki, a little bit. Tawni, of course, knew because of her close relationship with Paul's brother, Jeremy. But that was about it. It wasn't the same as having a boyfriend who showed up on her doorstep every other day. All Sierra had were letters that showed up every now and then, and she was usually the one who collected the mail. So no one knew how frequently Paul was writing her.

Standing in the hallway, Sierra felt lost. She didn't know exactly where to go. She probably shouldn't barge into her own room to put away the letter in case someone was trying to sleep. And she knew Granna Mae and possibly other people were in Granna Mae's room, so Sierra didn't feel comfortable barging in there. She opted for keeping the letter in her backpack, which hung on the coat rack downstairs.

Gently folding the onionskin sheet and sliding it into

her sweatshirt pocket, Sierra headed downstairs. The noise level rose with each step down. Just as she reached the entryway, the front door opened, and Wesley and Tawni stepped in.

"Hello!" Wesley greeted her, his booming voice sounding just like their father's.

Sierra received his warm hug and looked over his shoulder to see if his new girlfriend stood behind him. Only Tawni was there, shaking the rain off her jacket and smoothing back her long hair. The last time Sierra had seen her sister, Tawni's hair was a deep mahogany. Tonight it was white-blonde, a much lighter blonde than her natural color, and she wore long, layered bangs. She looked like a different person.

"Man," Tawni said, slipping off her coat before stepping all the way in. "When it rains here, it sure pours. What a night!"

"Oh, you don't know the half of it," Sierra murmured in her sister's ear as she reached out to hug her.

To Sierra's surprise, Tawni kissed her lightly on the cheek. This was new, too. Tawni had never been one to initiate affection. But she held Sierra close an extra moment and whispered, "I have something to tell you. Promise you won't tell anyone?"

Pulling away, Sierra looked into the face of her oh-so-changed sister and gave her an expectant expression. Tawni raised an eyebrow and tilted her head, waiting for Sierra to promise.

"I promise." Sierra whispered the words so not even

Wesley could hear them above the chatter in the living room and kitchen.

"Tawni, Wes!" Uncle Jack burst upon them and called over his shoulder to the rest of the group the glad announcement that the last of the clan had arrived.

The swarm of relatives buzzed toward them. Just before the lovely queen bee, Tawni, was swept up in their frenzy, she turned to Sierra and mouthed the word "Later."

chapter four

NO ONE SLEPT WELL IN THE JENSEN HOME THAT Thanksgiving eve night. Tyler's fever didn't break, and he woke up crying every few hours. Caleb couldn't sleep in the same room with Tyler, so he took his sleeping bag downstairs. Uncle Jack tripped over him when the older man went looking for a glass of milk sometime around three o'clock. Marshall had to go to the bathroom, causing the upstairs toilet to overflow again. He cried out frantically for his mom, and Sierra's dad appeared to help. But it didn't matter. The whole household was awake from all the commotion except, thankfully, Granna Mae, who had talked in her sleep between midnight and two o'clock, waking the five on her bedroom floor. Sierra had lain awake long hours, worrying that Granna Mae might get up in the middle of the night and stumble over one of them.

The night's fiascoes, mixed with the ceaseless rain and wailing winds, made for a houseful of grouchy people at breakfast. Everyone had a different story to tell about his or her experience in the night.

Sharon Jensen had risen early, or perhaps never went to bed by the look of the dark circles under her eyes. She put the huge turkey in the oven before dawn and managed to set enough coffee and bagels out on the counter to soothe the savage beasts that hunkered down the stairs. One thing the Jensens all liked was strong, black coffee. Mrs. Jensen kept the coffeemaker perking so the rich aroma filled the house.

Having had her fill of stories around the kitchen counter, Sierra slid past two of her aunts, who were insisting Sierra's mom give them something to do to help with the dinner. Sierra pulled a china cup and saucer from the cupboard and prepared a breakfast tray for Granna Mae.

Just as she placed the buttered toast and small tumbler of juice on the tray, her mother touched Sierra's arm and said, "Thank you, honey. May I assign Granna Mae to you for the next day or two? Make sure she gets her meals, okay? I thought I had that covered, but it's gotten away from me."

"Sure, I'll take care of her. Is there anything else you want me to do?"

"Just the dishes whenever you can. I'm sure I'll have the dishwasher running around the clock."

Sierra hated to do the dishes. She didn't know why; she just did. If she thought of doing them on her own and went about the task, it was no big deal. Then she felt she was helping out without being told. But if she was asked to do them, a spirit of rebellion rose inside her and whatever happiness she felt vanished.

This morning she clenched her jaw and forced herself

to smile and nod to her frenzied mother. Sierra knew deep down that it was the least she could do to help out, especially since she had done so little yesterday.

Sierra had to watch her every step on the way to Granna Mae's room. She successfully navigated the minefield of people's belongings and found Granna Mae dressed and making her bed. The white-haired soul appeared clear thinking and well rested.

"Oh, Lovey, you are too good to me." Granna Mae smoothed back the quilt and sat down at the little corner table Howard Jensen had built to make his mother's bedroom meals more convenient. It sat next to the window, covered with a floral tablecloth and set with the hen and rooster salt and pepper shakers that had resided faithfully on the kitchen counter for as long as anyone could remember.

Sierra placed the tray on the table and asked if she could bring anything else.

"No, no. This is wonderful. I imagine you're eager to spend time with all your cousins. You don't have to stay." Granna Mae picked up her favorite china cup and drew it to her lips with shaky hands.

Sierra realized she hadn't spent time with any of her relatives, since she had preferred to "be" with Paul the night before. The way she felt this morning, the only relative she wanted to talk to was Wesley, to find out why he hadn't brought home a guest. She also wanted to pry Tawni's big secret out of her. During the restless night, Sierra had made up lists of what the news could be. She narrowed it down to four possibilities: Tawni's going back to school, as Paul had written; hearing from her birth mother; becoming engaged to Jeremy; or landing a great modeling job. Tawni modeled full-time, but not every assignment was to her liking, such as a western-wear catalog shoot that had subjected her to country music for an entire day. And not every assignment paid well.

Sierra had considered coaxing the news from Tawni during one of the many awake sessions during the night, but then others in the room might have heard them. Besides, Tawni wasn't much of a night person.

But before Sierra knew it, the morning had fled, with Sierra running first downstairs to help out in the kitchen and then upstairs on some urgent errand and then back down the stairs, over and over again.

By two o'clock, the Jensen flock were gathered in the dining room and spilling over into the adjacent living room, where more tables were set up. The nicely browned turkey graced the center of the dining room table. The rain had stopped about an hour earlier, and weary autumn sunbeams tunneled their way through the clouds, weaving themselves through the lace curtains along the south side of the dining room. Only the bravest sunbeams made the long journey, and when they arrived on Granna Mae's best ivory linen tablecloth, they danced for joy among the cranberries and the mashed potatoes.

The Jensen family stood and held hands. Tyler was back to his sweet self and wanted to be next to Sierra to hold her hand. Katrina had blamed the fever and rough night on a molar that had broken through on the bottom right side of Tyler's mouth sometime in the night. Sierra wondered how mothers ever figured out these things.

Granna Mae stood at the head of the table, smiling contentedly and appearing delighted to have so many of her family members together. The merry sunbeams seemed to find her soft hair a pleasant place to end their journey, and there they stayed. Sierra smiled at the sight of her grandmother standing straight and still, oblivious to her beautiful "halo."

The rooms grew silent, and Granna Mae pronounced a blessing on the family. "May the Lord continue to show His grace and mercy to our family. May we live each day for Him with hearts full of love. And may we never cease to be thankful."

"Amen," one of the men echoed.

"Howard," Granna Mae said, turning to Sierra's dad, "would you do us the honor of giving thanks to our heavenly Father?"

"Sure. Let's pray."

As they bowed their heads, Mr. Jensen began to pray eloquently, as well as at length. The family had much for which to be thankful.

Sierra's chair was next to her mother's, close to the kitchen. As her father continued to pray, Sierra's nose picked up the scent of something burning. Dozens of fragrances had run through the house that day, but this was a new scent and not a pleasant one. Sierra let go of Tyler's hand and slipped into the kitchen. She checked the stove and saw that all the burners were turned off. Then she turned to the oven and noticed thin ribbons of smoke wafting through the door.

Grabbing a pot holder, she pulled open the door. Long flames rose from the pan of sweet potatoes and lunged toward her, hungry for the oxygen around her. Sierra let out a scream and put up her arm to block her face from the fire. Her mother appeared instantly and kicked the oven's door shut. It wasn't enough to contain the fire. The flames crawled up the cupboard, where Sierra's mom kept miscellaneous supplies that didn't fit in the pantry. Immediately, the stench of melting plastic filled the air. Sierra realized the arm of her sweater was smoking and pulled it off. She checked the arm of her turtleneck shirt. The flames hadn't gone through the sweater.

"Everyone out!" Sharon Jensen yelled. "We have a fire."

Pandemonium broke loose. Sierra felt her mother pushing her away from the oven and toward the back door.

Howard Jensen appeared in the kitchen and yelled, "Where's the fire extinguisher?"

"In the basement," his wife responded.

Sierra considered going after the extinguisher, but someone was pushing her out the back door. Everyone was talking and yelling at once. As soon as they burst through the door, Brutus leaped from his doghouse and barked and barked.

Wesley was behind Sierra. He seemed to be taking a head count. Some of the family had exited the front door, and two of the younger boys had run around to the back of the house and were excitedly asking, "Is the fire truck going to come?"

"Sierra," Wesley said, "run next door to call the fire department."

"We'll go with you," the two boys said.

Sierra didn't wait for them. She took off running. This all felt vaguely familiar. She had been the one to make the emergency call last spring in California when Christy's uncle Bob had been burned by a fire from an exploding gas barbecue. That experience helped Sierra keep her thoughts clear this time.

Mr. DeVries opened his front door before Sierra even reached his steps. "What's all the noise about?"

"Fire," was her simple explanation as she ran into his kitchen and dialed 911. Taking a deep breath, she calmly relayed the information. The fire trucks arrived in less than five minutes, and the family was ordered to cross the street. Everyone had a different theory on what had happened. Sierra repeated again exactly how she had discovered the fire. She scanned the group and breathed easier when she spotted Granna Mae. Her grandmother looked shaken, but Emma had her arm around the older woman's shoulders.

"It was the marshmallows on top of the sweet potatoes," Aunt Frieda explained to a group of neighbors who came bustling up to the Jensens. "Sharon put the tray back in the oven and set it on broil. She planned to brown those marshmallows for only a minute. Then we forgot and sat down to eat, and my brother had to pray the world's longest Thanksgiving prayer."

"You make it sound as though it was my dad's fault," Dillon said, stepping boldly between Aunt Frieda and the neighbor. "It wasn't his fault. It's an old house, and stuff in it breaks all the time. There was probably something wrong with the oven."

"I don't see any flames," Caleb said. "Can't we go back over there to see if they smashed down the door with their axes?"

"We'll wait until the firefighters tell us we can go back," Uncle Jack said. "Or until Howard comes out and waves us back."

Sierra froze. Where was her dad? Had he gone into the basement for the extinguisher? He hadn't gotten caught in the fire, had he? She scanned the growing clump of spectators. Neither her father nor her mother was in the crowd.

chapter five

"**WESLEY, WHERE ARE MOM AND DAD?**" SIERRA tugged on her brother's arm. The rain had begun again, and she shivered in her thin turtleneck. She had left her sweater on the kitchen floor.

"I thought they were here," he said, looking around.

"I haven't seen them," Sierra said. "What if they went down in the basement, and the firefighters don't know they're trapped?"

"Everyone else stay here," Wesley ordered, taking Sierra by the arm and running across the street in the rain.

Just as they reached the other side, a firefighter came out the front door and waved to the family members, indicating they could return.

"Where are my parents?" Sierra asked. "Are they okay?"

"They sure are. Thanks to them your house is okay—or at least most of your house. Your dad used a fire extinguisher to put out the fire. All we did was check for hot spots. Everything is okay. Looks like you folks will still have your Thanksgiving dinner, minus the yams and with a smoked turkey."

Some of the others who arrived in time to hear his comment chuckled, but Sierra thought the guy couldn't have made a worse joke.

Nearly an hour later, the family was ready to gather around the table again. Everyone had wanted to personally inspect the damage. The oven would need to be replaced and the cabinets over the oven rebuilt, but the fire hadn't spread elsewhere, which everyone considered amazing.

The smell was the awful part. Everything was permeated with the stench of smoke. All the windows and doors were open, and the heater ran full blast. Sierra laughed to herself when she looked around the table and noticed a number of relatives wearing their coats. Paul would have felt right at home. She couldn't wait to add a lengthy P.S. to her letter to him.

Howard Jensen prayed again. This time his prayer was a short but humbling one. Everyone agreed with the "Amen" as they realized even more vividly all they had to be thankful for.

The food was passed around with no attempt to warm it. Sharon Jensen had tried to put the food in the microwave in stages, but everyone convinced her it would be fine just the way it was. Howard Jensen carved, and everyone dished up. In shifty-eyed silence, they began to eat, each waiting for the others to say something.

Finally, Sharon Jensen put down her fork and said in a voice choked with tears, "This is awful! It all tastes like smoke." Then she burst out laughing.

The pressure seemed to release for all of them as they laughed, cried, and joked about the food along with Mrs.

Jensen. In the end, no one ate much except the olives, which for some reason didn't taste smoky. The entire dinner was sent to the trash cans outside instead of being neatly wrapped and stacked in the refrigerator, supplies for late-night turkey sandwiches.

The only salvageable part of the dinner was the pies. Mrs. Jensen had stored them in a large ice chest in the basement when she ran out of counter space in the kitchen. As she cut the pies, the doorbell rang, and one of the neighbors appeared with a pumpkin pie in her hand.

"We had an extra pie, and I thought maybe it would help, with the fire and everything."

"Thanks," Sharon Jensen said graciously. "We were just about to serve dessert."

Before the pie was served, another neighbor came by. This one delivered a plateful of sliced turkey and two pumpkin pies. Mrs. Jensen thanked her and added the pumpkin pies to the seven already lining the counter.

"Years from now we'll all look back and remember this as the year we ate pumpkin pie and nothing else," she said as Sierra watched her cut the generous slices.

After the feast of pumpkin pies, two whole pies were left. The table was being cleared when the doorbell rang and another neighbor stood there, offering a bowl of left-over stuffing and two pumpkin pies.

"None of us had room for pie," the neighbor stated. "I thought maybe your family could put them to good use."

Sierra heard her dad thank the woman and then deliver the goods to the kitchen counter.

"It seems for every pie we eat, another one shows up," Wes said.

"And to think I knocked myself out making all those pies yesterday," Mrs. Jensen said, and she burst into another round of laughter and tears.

Even though Sierra had planned to sneak upstairs to write Paul, she decided she should stay to help her mom before she fell apart completely. For almost two hours, she washed everything that was handed to her. The kitchen's entire contents reeked of smoke and needed to be cleaned. All the aunts seemed to enjoy hunting out the smoke-tainted items. They celebrated their discoveries by delivering them to Sierra saying, "Ew! Smell this plate" or "Phew! This candleholder really stinks!" Sierra kept washing, emptying the sink, filling it with more soapy water, and washing some more.

For a while Aunt Emma dried dishes. Then Sierra's mom took over. Wesley came in at the end of the first hour, as if they were part of a tag team. He said there was a request for more coffee from the living room. That got Mrs. Jensen away from the sink long enough for him to pick up a towel and work on the row of glasses Sierra was washing. Aunt Frieda insisted that all the shelves be wiped off before anything could be returned, so the glasses had to wait until she was ready for them. She also took on the task of taking down the curtains to be washed.

Sierra's cousin Molly had been assigned by her mother, Frieda, to wipe down the walls, the top of the refrigerator, and the cupboards. The only problem was that Molly kept dunking her sponge into Sierra's dishwater. Instantly, the water would turn sooty gray. It was driving Sierra crazy. She knew everything needed to be washed off, but why couldn't Molly use the paper towels and spray cleaner as Mrs. Jensen had suggested and Sierra kept reinforcing? Wesley solved the problem by providing Molly with a mixing bowl full of sudsy water and a new sponge.

"I heard you were thinking of bringing a guest home for Thanksgiving," Sierra said to Wesley. "I bet you're glad now you didn't bring her."

"Her?" Wesley said. He shook his head. "I invited a guy from Japan. He had never heard of our American custom of Thanksgiving. But he decided to go with someone who lives in Corvallis rather than be gone all weekend with me. I'm sure he'll be sorry he missed all the excitement here."

"Rats," Sierra said. "I thought for sure you were bringing home a girlfriend."

"Nope, not me."

"No interesting women at school this year?" Sierra asked.

"Plenty of interesting women. Just not the right one."

"What would make her the right one?" Molly asked.

"I have a list," Wes said quietly.

"A real list?" Molly asked. "A written-out list?"

Wes turned to her and nodded. "Don't you?"

"Well, in my head, yeah, but nothing on paper."

"Put it on paper," Wes challenged. "It will help to clarify what you're looking for."

"Like, what do you put down?" Molly was short with round glasses and an upturned nose. She was usually so quiet that Sierra was surprised to hear her quizzing Wes.

"Character and personality qualities, life goals, you know. It's not a physical shopping list: five foot two, eyes of blue, or anything like that."

"Give me an example of one of the things on your list," Molly prodded.

Wesley hesitated. "Well, she has to be a believer and have a growing relationship with the Lord."

"What else?"

Wesley looked at Sierra, and with a teasing smile he said, "I'd like someone who is emotionally healthy. Preferably an emotional virgin."

"A what?" Molly wrinkled up her nose.

"You know, a woman who has been saving her heart for the right guy. Someone who hasn't been falling in and out of love since she was 12 and now, at 23, is a big tangle of broken pieces from her past relationships."

"You're a dreamer," Molly said with a shake of her head. She was a year younger than Sierra but had always acted more mature and serious than her cousin. "No girls like that are left. Especially by the time they're 23."

"Oh, I don't know," Wes said, giving Sierra another grin. "Some 17-year-olds have managed to guard their hearts. A guy can always hope a few wise women don't come with a truckload of emotional baggage when they're ready to start a serious relationship."

"What about you?" Aunt Emma said, jumping into the discussion. "Can you honestly say you're emotionally damage-free? I seem to remember a certain young beauty who showed up at Christmas one year when you were in high school."

"I never said I was an emotional virgin." Wes turned and leaned against the counter, his hands resting on the tile as if he were bracing himself for the verbal onslaught that was sure to come from this roomful of women.

"Isn't that just like a man?" Aunt Frieda spouted. "They want the woman to be perfect, but they don't think they have to be."

"I didn't say that," Wesley stated. "It's just my ideal. I do understand reality."

"How could you if you're 23 and still carrying around a list of requirements?" Aunt Frieda was the only one in the family who had been through a divorce. She had let everyone know that she had felt unprepared for a realistic marriage because she believed all she had to do was marry someone who said he was a Christian.

For the next 10 minutes, Frieda challenged Wesley to adjust his thinking to a more realistic view. She emphasized the scriptures that said Christians are supposed to love one another and help the weaker ones along. "Not a single verse says we should marry only people who are completely pure because, if you haven't noticed, no one fits that description. We all fail. True love means sticking by the other person in his or her failures and loving that person no matter what."

Wesley didn't argue with that but added, "What about 1 Peter where it says we're to live holy lives?"

"We all fail," Frieda insisted. " 'Holy' means complete, doesn't it? We're made complete when we surrender our lives to Christ. He's the one who makes us 'holy.' It has nothing to do with emotional baggage."

"I think it does," Wes said. "We have choices every day of what we choose to keep in the storehouse of our hearts. All I'm saying is I'd like to meet a woman who has relatively few boxes of explosives in her storehouse."

Molly laughed, which helped break some of the tension that had been building. Sierra had finished the last dish and wanted to get out of there. She felt warm from the dishwater. She also felt a little nervous that Wesley might use her again as an example of someone with a storehouse full of empty boxes. That wasn't true. She had collected a few emotional mementos along the way. She had told Wes about some of them, like Drake and Alex. Wes had never suggested to her that he saw anything emotionally inappropriate in those relationships.

But Wes didn't know much about the box marked "Paul," which now filled the storehouse of Sierra's heart. She thought of Wes as understanding how special that relationship was to her. But in reality, how could he? He hadn't been home for weeks. He probably didn't even know she and Paul were corresponding.

Slipping out of the kitchen and pulling her green back-pack off the coat rack in the entryway, Sierra retreated to Granna Mae's room. To her surprise, the bedroom was empty. She pulled out Paul's photo, which was tucked in the bottom of her mound of now untidy clothes. He was still smiling at her, even though he had that tiny slice above his heart.

She stared at the picture for a long time and wished

Paul were here right now. They would go for a long walk together, hand-in-hand. It wouldn't matter that the rain fell on them or that the wet, molding leaves would fly against their legs. They would be together—close together. To Sierra that's all that mattered.

If she couldn't hold Paul's hand, she at least had his picture and his words. And she could give him back her words. In the solitude, Sierra pulled out a piece of notebook paper and wrote at the top:

P.S. This will probably be the longest P.S. you've ever seen. It might even be the longest one in the world. It's been less than 24 hours since I wrote you, but you're not going to believe what happened here today.

Sierra twirled the end of the pen across her smiling lips and thought how, in a small, secret way, she was spending time alone with Paul. Even with a house full of company.

chapter six

"**I**S EVERYONE IN?" SHARON JENSEN LOOKED OVER her shoulder from the driver's seat of the family van. All of the passenger seats held Jensen women, seat-belted and ready for an outing that was, in Sierra's opinion, more important to her mom than to anyone else. It was Friday afternoon, the final day of the reunion, and her mom was determined to take all the women to tea in downtown Portland.

Sierra had resisted going. It had been another restless night for everyone, and Sierra wanted to sleep in. She had to work Saturday, and Sunday was filled with church and activities, so this was her only real day of vacation. Even though she had spent little time with her relatives because she kept finding quiet corners to write to Paul, Sierra enjoyed the isolation. She knew she was related to these people, but right now, at this point in her life, she wasn't interested in them.

Granna Mae was in the front passenger seat, and Tawni and Sierra were wedged in the back with Aunt Frieda, who had a wide berth. Frieda was leaning forward, chattering with Aunt Emma in the next seat up. Sierra's teen cousins, Molly and Nicole, were playing a finger yarn game with the seven-year-old twins, Amanda and Kayla.

"Tell me your big news," Sierra said, leaning close to Tawni so no one else could hear. "I didn't get a chance to ask you yesterday."

Tawni had pulled her hair back in a stylish twist. The strands framing Tawni's face tickled Sierra's nose when she leaned close to her sister's ear.

"I've decided to go back to college in January," Tawni announced.

"That's what Paul said you were thinking about."

Tawni looked surprised. "When did Paul talk to you? And how did he know?"

"Jeremy told him, of course. And I haven't talked to Paul. He told me in a letter. We've been writing each other. A lot," she added for emphasis.

Tawni picked up the clue and looked pleasantly surprised. "Jeremy hadn't told me. Are you and Paul e-mail buddies?"

"No."

"No? You write pen-and-paper letters?"

Sierra nodded. The van went over a bump as Mrs. Jensen drove onto the Hawthorne Bridge. The vehicle carried the yakking band of women through the pouring rain toward the heart of the city.

"I'm impressed," Tawni said. "I didn't realize you two were, well, what are you? Dating by mail?"

Sierra smiled. She liked that. "I guess you could call it that."

"How often do you write?"

With a shrug, Sierra said, "I don't know. Every day. Every other day. Sometimes twice a day."

Tawni's blue eyes grew wide. "This is serious, little sister. Why didn't you tell me? Why didn't Jeremy tell me? Do you think Paul has told him?"

"I don't know," Sierra said. She suddenly felt a pinch in her stomach. What if Paul hadn't said anything because he didn't think it was that big a deal? What if their correspondence was only a big deal to her? But how could that be? The guy was composing poetry for her and sitting alone on Friday nights, talking to her on paper. Sierra tried to bolster her confidence. Of course this relationship was as important to Paul as it was to her. He had made that clear plenty of times—hadn't he?

"Maybe you shouldn't say anything to Jeremy," Sierra said cautiously. "I mean, if Paul wants to tell him, brother to brother, I wouldn't want to steal his thunder."

"You mean like Paul stole mine by telling you I'm going to Reno?" Tawni said.

"What do you mean, going to Reno? I thought you said you were going back to school."

"I am. At the University of Nevada, Reno." Tawni looked like a woman whose mind and will were set in stone.

"Why Reno? What about Jeremy? Why don't you go to school in San Diego, where you live? I mean, what about all your modeling opportunities? Who do you know in Reno, of all places?"

"No one yet," Tawni said with a sly edge to her voice.

"I don't get it," Sierra said. "Is Jeremy transferring there?"

"No. He has only one semester left. He graduates next June, just like Wes. Jeremy figures he can live through his final semester without me. He even thinks his grades might improve."

"Do Mom and Dad know about this?"

"Not yet. I'm keeping it a secret until I receive the acceptance papers. There have been some small problems with my transcripts."

"I still don't get why you would go to a university where you don't know anyone and you're out-of-state so you'll have to pay more."

Tawni just smiled. "Maybe and maybe not."

Before Sierra could extract any more information from her sister, Mrs. Jensen pulled the van into a parking space and turned off the engine. "I have several umbrellas here," she said, offering the Portland essential gear to everyone.

Sierra looked out, and the first shop window she saw had the words "Carla's Café" printed in gold letters under the scalloped, striped awning. She smiled and nudged Tawni. "Did you know we were going to Carla's? This is the place you brought Paul and me that night before he left for Scotland."

"We're not going there," Tawni said. "Mom found another place around the corner. It's an old hotel that serves high tea in a separate parlor. Didn't you hear her talking about it this morning? The parlor still has a lot of the original furniture from when the hotel opened for business in the late 1800s."

"I guess I didn't hear her," Sierra said, scooting across the seat. She stepped onto the sidewalk with the happy, chattering women and cast a melancholy gaze at the front window of the café. Someday she hoped Paul and she could return to sit by the front window. Their conversation would be different now. Paul wouldn't have to ask if she had a crush on him. He would know, as she knew, that what they had was much more than a childish crush.

"Sierra," Tawni called, "are you coming with us?"

The others had already scurried down the street and disappeared around the corner. Sierra stood alone in front of Carla's with the rain dampening her hair. She didn't mind. She had gotten much wetter than this one day last February when she was walking home with a big bouquet of daffodils as a gift for Granna Mae. She was soaked then, and Paul had seen her while driving by with his friends. That's when he had started calling her the Daffodil Queen.

"I'm coming," Sierra said, still lost in her dream world and not caring at all about sitting around with a bunch of relatives for a tea party. She would much rather go inside Carla's and sit in the chair she had sat in last time and imagine Paul sitting across from her. She could dream up all the things they would talk about and the way he would reach across the table to take her hand. He would squeeze it gently and smile in a way that would say, "I'm so happy we're finally together, Sierra."

She sighed as she rounded the corner, with Tawni three steps ahead, holding her umbrella close to the top of her head to protect her perfect hairdo. Mrs. Jensen had asked that Sierra dress up, and she had managed to put together an outfit consisting of a long skirt, a pair of warm socks, and her dad's old cowboy boots. Her long, wheat-colored sweater hung over the brown and cream straight skirt. She was keenly aware that her outfit wasn't dressy and stylish like Tawni's. But Sierra felt like Sierra: comfortable, unpretentious, original.

Now, if she could only convince Aunt Frieda to stop giving her disapproving looks she would be fine. Fine enough to almost enjoy this tea party—for her mother's sake, if nothing else.

The parlor of the old hotel was charming. The women were seated in groups of four at several small, round tables that were arranged on the same side of the room as a baby grand piano. When they entered and took their seats, the pianist played Beethoven's "For Elise," which had always been one of Sierra's favorites. She sat next to Granna Mae, and the twins took the other two chairs.

A waiter appeared wearing a white shirt and black vest, with a towel over his arm. He explained the delicacies that were being served that afternoon and went through the list of available teas. Sierra ordered an Oregon specialty tea, marionberry. It came in a china pot with a silver strainer, since it was leaf tea and not in a bag. The twins loved all the attention given to dainty details: the decorated sugar cubes, the tiny silver creamers, and the cucumber sandwiches cut in star and heart shapes. The hotel even served pumpkin pie in cube-sized squares with dots of thick whipped cream on top.

"I don't want my pumpkin squares," Amanda said. "I'm kind of tired of pumpkin pie."

"Me, too," Kayla said.

"That's okay," Sierra assured them. "You don't have to eat the pumpkin pie if you don't want to. I'm kind of pumpkin-pied-out myself." She knew she wasn't the only one who had eaten a slice of cold pie that morning. Wesley had joined her, and so had their dad.

Granna Mae participated warmly, acknowledging when she was spoken to, but not always having an answer. Sierra could tell this was one of those times when Granna Mae's mind was beginning to slip through the fragile fingers of reality and slide into a world of confusion.

"This cranberry nut bread is very good," Sierra said to her. "Do you like it?"

Granna Mae smiled politely as if she had no idea who Sierra was or why she was talking to Granna Mae. She ate, which Sierra considered a good thing because when she had brought breakfast up to her grandmother that morning, she had only nibbled on the toast. Sierra now poured some English Breakfast blend through the strainer into Granna Mae's cup.

"More sugar for you?" Sierra asked, looking for some kind of response, any kind of response.

"Can I do it?" Amanda asked. She turned to Granna Mae and said, "One lump or two?"

It was obvious the twins would long remember this experience, and Sierra almost felt glad she had come along to play "little girl" again.

"One, please," Granna Mae responded to Amanda, stirring the tea in her cup with a fairly steady hand.

The girls grew restless before the older women did, and

Sierra offered to take them to the hotel gift shop. They left Granna Mae with Mrs. Jensen and Tawni and off they went, Sierra in her rather un-tea-partyish outfit, and her twin cousins in their pretty party dresses, with starched bows in their hair. The girls each took one of Sierra's hands and nearly skipped with joy at the special attention they were getting.

"When I grow up, I'm going to dress just like you," Amanda said. "You're cool, Sierra."

"I want to be just like you, too," Kayla agreed. "I want to go to Europe like you do all the time, too."

"I don't go all the time," Sierra said.

"My mom said you did. She said you went twice this year because you're a free spirit."

"Kayla," Amanda scolded, "you make it sound like a bad thing."

"No I don't. Mom said she was a free spirit, too, before she married."

"Aunt Emma said that?" Sierra asked as they entered the gift shop.

"Yes," both girls answered in unison.

Sierra smiled. "You have a very cool mother, you know."

Kayla shrugged. "I guess. But not as cool as you."

Sierra and her little fan club began to poke around in the charming gift shop. One antique table was covered with a collection of teapots and other tea goodies from England. A red plaid tin of Scottish shortbread caught Sierra's eye, and she was glad she had stuck a $20 bill in her boot. It served as her purse when she didn't feel like carrying her backpack. She thought about buying some shortbread cookies to eat while she sipped a cup of tea and wrote her next letter to Paul.

She had finished the long letter with the even longer P.S., which she had added to several times, and had slapped two airmail stamps on it because it was so thick. Even now it sat in the mailbox waiting for the postal worker to pick it up.

"Look at these sewing kits," Kayla said, lifting a needlepoint kit up to Sierra. It came from a basket at Sierra's feet where dozens of small stitching kits were marked half-off.

"That's nice," Sierra said, only glancing at the Scottish crest that said "MacIver" across the top of the package. "Do you like to embroider?"

"I do," Kayla said. "Amanda doesn't. But this is ugly. They should have flowers or something."

Sierra glanced at the package again and saw what Kayla meant. The MacIver clan crest was a circle with a boar's head in the middle. She made a face at Kayla and said, "Yikes! Who would want to embroider that?"

Returning her attention to the lovely china cups, cookie tins, and small silver teaspoons, Sierra noticed a tin of Scottish Breakfast tea. She knew that would be the perfect tea to go with her shortbread. Collecting her private tea-party fixings, Sierra shuffled toward the register. But then the MacIver crest floated through her thoughts, and she suddenly turned around.

"Kayla, did they have any other Scottish clan crests in that basket of needlepoint kits?"

Kayla nodded, and Sierra dove into the basket, a woman on a mission. If she could find Paul MacKenzie's family crest, she would have her problem solved of what to buy him for Christmas. She could embroider the crest and frame it for him. Paul would love it. As long as it wasn't something disgusting like a boar's head.

chapter seven

SIERRA FILED THROUGH THE BASKET OF NEEDLEPOINT kits, searching for "MacKenzie." She found one at the back of the basket. Drawing it close, she studied the crest. It was a mountain with three pillars of flames rising from it. For a fleeting moment she thought it looked like the flaming sweet potatoes and marshmallows she had battled in the oven yesterday. The Latin words surrounding the mountain were *"Lucero non uro."*

"I wonder what that means," Sierra muttered as she triumphantly rose with the prize in her hand. She had enough money for the needlepoint, cookies, and tea, but her change back was only seven cents. "Good thing we don't have any sales tax in Oregon," she said to Kayla and Amanda. "Otherwise I would have had to borrow some money from you. "

"Why did you buy that? Are you going to sew it?" Amanda asked.

"Yes. It's going to be a gift for someone who is very special to me. And this is that person's last name." She pulled the kit from the bag. "MacKenzie." Sierra loved the way the name rolled off her tongue.

"What's that supposed to be?" Amanda asked, pointing to the crest.

"A mountain on fire, I guess," Sierra said. She gave Kayla and Amanda a big smile. "It's a whole lot better than a pig's head, don't you think?"

They laughed. Sierra enjoyed her little cousins.

"Do you think the moms are ready to go yet?" she asked.

"Not our mom. She's always the last one to leave anywhere. There's always just one more person she wants to talk to," Kayla said.

"That's how it is with us free spirits," Sierra replied. "We always have one more person we want to talk to."

The only person Sierra wanted to talk to at the moment was Paul. She wished she could prepare a proper tea party for him with her shortbread and Scottish Breakfast tea. The thought stayed with her and formulated into a plan.

As the group of Jensen women scurried to the van through the rain-drenched streets, Sierra's plan came together. For Christmas she could send Paul a tea party in a box. All he would have to do is open each of the little wrapped boxes in order, according to the number on them. First the tea, but not Scottish or British tea. She would buy some Oregon marionberry tea or maybe some Coffee People coffee beans, which were big in Oregon. She would write out instructions for him to start the coffee or tea while he opened the other gifts. Then he would unwrap the goodies. They should be from the Northwest. Maybe some smoked salmon or honey biscuits with blackberry jam.

The more Sierra mulled her plan over, the more excited she grew. This could be fun. She would include a long letter in the box, of course, and the finished clan crest—and what else? Maybe a picture of her. Yes! That would be perfect. A little window for Paul to look into her world and watch her face as he read her words.

"Are you even listening to me?" Tawni said, poking Sierra's arm as they sat squeezed together in the back of the van.

"What did you say?"

"I asked what you bought in the gift shop."

"Oh. I bought some tea and cookies." For some reason she hesitated to tell Tawni about the MacKenzie needlepoint. Would she think it was a silly idea? Jeremy was obviously a MacKenzie, too. Would Tawni wish she had gotten one for Jeremy? There was only this one MacKenzie kit in the store.

"Is that all?"

"Well, I also bought something you might think is dumb, so, if you do, don't say anything, okay?"

"Why would I say anything?"

"Just don't, okay?"

"Okay."

Sierra pulled the kit from the bag and showed it to her sister with no explanation.

"You're going to sew that?"

"Sure. It can't be too hard. Don't you think it will make a great Christmas present for Paul?"

"You're going to finish that by Christmas?"

"Yes," Sierra said defensively. "It's not very big."

"Yes, but look at all those tiny stitches. Don't they call that petit point? I'd never have the patience to attempt something like that."

At least I don't have to worry about Tawni wanting to steal my gift idea, Sierra thought.

"Well, have fun," Tawni said flatly. "If you don't finish it before Christmas, you could always send him a framed picture of yourself."

"I was thinking of doing that, too," Sierra said. She wondered if her mom had told Tawni that Paul had sent her a picture for her birthday.

"That's what I'm giving Jeremy. I have some good shots from one of the photographers, and I thought I'd have several framed while I'm here. I'll give Jeremy the best one and send one to Mom and Dad."

Sierra considered Tawni's giving away professional model shots different from her own idea of taking a picture in the backyard. She wanted to send a little window to Paul, not plaster a billboard across his room.

She noticed the writing on the back of the stitchery kit and held it close to read the fine print. "Listen to this," she said, reading aloud to Tawni. " 'The MacKenzie clan claims to be descended from Colin, progenitor of the Earl of Ross. He died in 1278 and was succeeded by his son Kenneth.' "

"In 1278?" Tawni questioned.

"That's what it says."

"How amazing that anyone could trace his history back that far. Or at least people whom he knows he is descended from." Tawni let out a noticeable sigh.

Sierra decided to let it go. Every now and then Tawni would become depressed over being adopted and not knowing where she came from genetically. A few months ago, Tawni had tracked down her birth mother and had written her a letter. Tawni hadn't heard anything back. Even though Tawni had said she felt the important point was that she had written the letter, Sierra could tell at this moment that Tawni felt discouraged. Sierra decided to plunge ahead and read the rest of the MacKenzie history.

" 'The clan crest is a mountain inflamed with the motto *"Lucero non uro,"* which is translated, "I shine, not burn." MacKenzie also uses the crest badge of a stag's head and the motto *"Cuidich 'n righ,"* which is translated, "Help the king." The Gaelic name is "MacCoinnich." ' "

"Sierra," Tawni snapped, "I get the point. MacKenzie is a Scottish name. All right. Why are you obsessing over this?"

"I'm not. I just thought you would be interested in the history of Jeremy's family."

"That's only on his father's side," Tawni said. "He's part whatever his mother is, you know. And so is Paul. There's such a dilution of nationalities over the years, nobody can really say they're completely French or Scottish or whatever."

Tawni's words were so sharp that Sierra decided to slip the needlepoint kit back into the bag and change the subject. All she could figure was that if Tawni couldn't identify her birth heritage, then no one else should be able to.

But Tawni's lack of support didn't diminish Sierra's

enthusiasm in starting on the project as soon as they reached home. She went up to Granna Mae's room, where her grandmother was lying down. Sierra curled up in the chair by the window, and as the raindrops pattered against the pane, she quietly hummed and began her project. She had never done anything like this before. But she could read directions, and she could thread a needle. Everything was included in the kit. How hard could this be?

The next day, Saturday, at work, Sierra pulled out her needlepoint during her afternoon break. She was determined to get a lot done because the night before she had been persuaded by her parents to participate in the hour-long good-bye to their holiday guests, and after that the massive cleanup began. She didn't crawl into bed until after eleven, but at least it was in her own bed, and her room was the cleanest it had been in months, thanks to Tawni's diligent assistance.

Sierra worked at Mama Bear's Bakery, known for its cinnamon rolls. When the weather was cold and rainy, as it had been lately, Mama Bear's was packed with customers seeking comfort in a steaming cup of espresso and a warm, gooey cinnamon roll. Since the place was filled with customers this Saturday, Sierra's break was shorter than usual. The owner, Mrs. Kraus, frantically asked Sierra to bring more coffee beans out of the storage room. The needlepoint project was stuffed into her backpack.

Sierra didn't pull it out again until that night. Removing herself from the rest of the family, she hid in her room, trying to line up the tiny stitches. On the way home from work, she had bought a new frame to get the right size glass to replace the broken glass in Paul's picture. She also had bought some wrapping paper and a roll of film. If the rain cleared tomorrow after church, Sierra planned to find someone to take pictures of her.

But the rain continued. Mr. Jensen took everyone out for lunch after the service. Sierra was starving, having eaten only a slice of pumpkin pie for breakfast as they ran out the door for church. Gavin and Wesley had done the same thing. The family was down to only one pumpkin pie.

Sierra ate her lunch quickly and then sat there, wishing she could get back to her needlepoint. She decided she needed to always carry it with her. That way she could work on it at times like this, while everyone else sat around the table talking. Actually, she found it pleasant to be back to just the immediate family of her mom and dad, Wes, Tawni, Sierra, Gavin, Dillon, and Granna Mae. A crowd still, but a comfortable, familiar crowd.

Mrs. Jensen was saying something about the family going skiing during Christmas vacation or maybe during a long weekend in January.

"If we went in January, we could go to Tahoe," Sierra suggested. "That way we would have a free place to stay with Tawni in Reno."

"In Reno?" her mom said. "Why would Tawni be in Reno?"

All eyes went to Tawni, who was giving Sierra a furious, icy stare. Sierra suddenly remembered that Tawni had said she was waiting to tell her parents about her plans.

Sierra pursed her lips together and reached her hand

across the table to touch her sister's arm. "I'm sorry. I forgot."

Tawni still looked mad.

"You heard from Lina?" Mrs. Jensen said slowly to Tawni.

Then it all became clear to Sierra. Tawni's birth mother, Lina Rasmussen, lived in Reno. She was a professor at the university. That was all Tawni knew about her.

"No," Tawni said quietly, drawing in a deep breath through her flared nostrils.

Mr. Jensen leaned in, next to his wife. His skin began to wrinkle between his eyebrows. "Do you want to talk about this, honey?"

Tawni looked away for a moment and then turned back, taking them all in with her composed gaze. She almost seemed to have switched to a different face, one that was ready for the camera.

"There's not much to talk about," Tawni said. "I've applied to go to school in January at the University of Nevada, Reno. I haven't been accepted yet, so I wasn't going to say anything until it was official."

"This is a surprise," her dad said. "I'd feel more comfortable with these kinds of big decisions if you would talk to your mother and me first."

"There wasn't anything to talk about."

"Don't do that," Wesley said, jumping in with his big-brother voice. "Don't pull away, Tawni. We all know you're going through this thing about your birth mom, and we've supported your searching for her and contacting her. But if you haven't heard from her and you're thinking of just showing up on her doorstep, or worse, enrolling in one of her classes, I think that's a pretty big deal, and you should talk with us about it."

Tawni looked shocked. "Is that what you think? You think I'm going to UNR to stalk Lina or something? I'm going because they have the kinds of courses I'm interested in. I can't believe you guys are all against me on this."

The tension was thick around the table, and Sierra felt it was her fault.

Then the waitress appeared with a smile and said, "Did anyone leave room for pumpkin pie?"

"No!" they all answered in sharp unison.

chapter eight

SIERRA FELT MISERABLE. SHE KNEW TAWNI HAD BEEN invited to have Thanksgiving with Jeremy's family in San Diego, but she had chosen to come to Portland because all the family was gathering and her parents had paid for her flight home. Sierra wondered now if her sister wished she had gone to Jeremy's instead, or at least had coaxed Jeremy to come home with her and support her in this Reno decision.

After lunch, Tawni had to catch her flight back to San Diego. The whole family was in the van when they dropped Tawni off at Portland International Airport. Tawni politely and sweetly said good-bye to each of them with the expected hug. But a chill was in the air instead of the warmth with which Tawni had greeted them a few days before.

"I'm sorry," Sierra whispered again as they hugged. "Please forgive me." Sierra had tried to remember if Tawni had specifically told Sierra not to say anything or if it had only been implied. It didn't matter. Tawni was mad. It would take a while for her to melt.

"I forgive you." Tawni said the words, but they stung as much as if she had said, "You're such a brat." Their relationship hadn't been this awful for years.

When Sierra reached home, Vicki called and said a bunch of Sierra's friends were going out that night. Sierra would have loved to get out of the house, away from family, and be with her friends for a few hours. But she had made a commitment to help out that night at the Highland House with its new teen hot line. She knew she couldn't cancel, so she told Vicki she couldn't go. Immediately, she began to feel sorry for herself. Randy, Vicki, and the rest of her friends were going to have one last blast of fun before returning to school, while Sierra was going to be responsible and do her duty. It was a bitter pill to swallow.

Her only consolation was that maybe the phones wouldn't ring much, and she could spend the time working on her needlepoint. To add to her unhappiness, she was concerned that the day was nearly gone, and she hadn't gotten any pictures taken. She needed to start on that project right away. Maybe tomorrow.

Only a few people were at the Highland House when she arrived. Parking in back, she hurried to the office. The director, Uncle Mac, was there with a college-age girl, and they both were on the phones when Sierra walked in. Uncle Mac waved and motioned for her to go to the third phone, which was located in a small cubicle against the wall. The Highland House had started this outreach a few months earlier, and their facilities and resources were limited. That's why Sierra wanted to help. With her work and school schedule, she didn't have much time to volunteer, and this hot-line program seemed to be the best way to contribute to the Highland House's work.

Taking off her jacket and settling into the cubicle, Sierra put her Bible, her notes from the training course, and her needlepoint on the table in front of her. She had just threaded the needle when the phone rang. Glancing out of the cubicle, she saw Uncle Mac motion for her to pick it up, since he was still on a call, as was the other girl. Sierra reached for the phone on the second ring.

"Highland House Teen Hot Line," she answered. "This is Sierra."

Her heart began to race. Even after all the training she had received on how to respond to the calls that came into this homeless shelter, she felt uneasy about how this, her first call, would go.

"I read one of your brochures," said the female voice on the other end of the line. "The one on purity."

"Yes?" Sierra was familiar with the brochure. It explained the health reasons for abstinence and included some verses from the Bible about purity.

"Well, I have a question."

From the girl's voice, Sierra guessed she was around Sierra's age or younger. That was the strength of the teen hot-line program, according to Uncle Mac. Teens were more willing to talk to another teen than to an adult when it came to certain problems.

"I was wondering," the girl said slowly. "I mean, I agree with what this brochure says about being pure and saving yourself for marriage and everything, but what if . . ." Her voice faltered. Sierra thought the girl was crying.

"Yes?" Sierra prodded gently.

"What if you're not pure? What if . . ." The voice broke into a sob.

"It's okay," Sierra said. She flipped through her training notes until she found the paper marked "Purity."

"What if," the girl asked, "you want to be like that—pure, I mean—but it's already too late?"

"I understand," Sierra said. "It's okay."

"I can only stay on the phone for a few more minutes," the girl said. "Is there anything you can tell me?"

Sierra drew in a breath of courage. "You're right, you can only have one 'first time,' but there is a way to start over. Not physically, but you can become clean in God's eyes.

"As you probably found out when you lost your virginity, you lost a piece of your heart, too. But God made a way to refill that emptiness. In 1 John 1:9, the Bible says that 'if we confess our sins, He is faithful and righteous to forgive us our sins and to cleanse us from all unrighteousness.' "

Sierra looked up from her notes and tried to make her answer to this caller sound more natural. "In people terms, all we have to do is admit to God that we messed up and that we need Him to forgive us. After that, He keeps His end of the deal and washes those messes from His memory. By doing all of this, God fills the empty holes we created by loaning or giving our hearts to things besides Him."

The caller didn't say anything. Sierra looked up at the wall and glanced at the sign over the bulletin board.

"At the Highland House," she said to the caller in as

gentle a voice as possible, "our motto is, 'A safe place for a fresh start,' and that's exactly what Jesus is willing to offer you. He'll give you a second chance to be pure. You may not feel you're pure in the way you read about in our brochure, but remember, God sees a new, spotless you."

Then speaking almost as rapidly as she felt her heart was beating, Sierra finished with, "To start 'secondary virginity,' make a commitment to yourself, to God, and to your future mate. Promise that the next time you have sex will be after you're married. Don't settle for less than God's best for you."

There was silence on the other end. For a moment Sierra worried that the caller had hung up and that all her advice had evaporated into thin air.

"Do you really believe all that?" the caller asked.

"Yes, of course," Sierra answered quickly.

"I mean, did you just read that, or do you really agree with what you said?"

"I believe it," Sierra said firmly. "I agree with it because everything God says is true. If He promises to make us clean when we come to Him asking for forgiveness, then that's what He does. It's based on His promises and His Word. Not on what we feel."

"Well, I have to go," the caller said. "Thanks. I need some time to think about what you said."

"Call any time."

A click sounded on the other end, and Sierra's heart sank. She would have felt so much better if the caller had said, "Oh, thank you so much! That's exactly what I needed to hear. I'm going to pray right now, and I know everything will be better." Instead, the click of the line going dead echoed in Sierra's ear.

Two hours later, when her shift ended, she talked to Uncle Mac about how she felt. The next six calls had gone about the same.

"The first call I took was the hardest, though," Sierra said. "It made me feel as though I didn't know what I was doing. I mean, I have the answers here and here," Sierra said, pointing to her head and to the notebook in front of her. "And I believe them here." She patted her heart. "But it has to be hard to see things clearly when you're caught in the middle of a situation."

Uncle Mac nodded. "It is hard. We're complex human beings. It's not just our minds or our bodies that direct us. We have complicated emotions and that blessed and cursed free will God gave us. We choose every day, all day long, what we want to do."

"I know, but what if someone didn't choose for herself? What about the first caller I had? All she said was that she wasn't pure like the Highland House brochure described. What if that hadn't been her choice? I mean, what if she had been, you know, raped? I was going through the information on asking forgiveness, but what if it wasn't her choice that she wasn't a virgin anymore?"

Uncle Mac nodded knowingly. "First she needs to know she didn't do anything wrong. Did you give her the 800 number in the back of the manual for the sexual abuse counseling service?"

Sierra bit her lower lip and shook her head. "I forgot."

"You'll remember next time. It takes a while to become

familiar with all the material and remember what to say in each situation. There's no sense worrying about it now. Trust that God used your willing heart as you talked to her and pray that He'll lead her to the next step."

With a sigh, Sierra said, "This is a lot harder than I thought it was going to be. Each situation is different, isn't it?"

"Yes, and each person is different. That's how God sees us: unique and wonderfully made. He works in each heart and life in a different way. The only sure direction, the only true answer to any problem, is to come to God and turn everything over to Him."

Uncle Mac gave Sierra a few more pointers and thanked her for volunteering her time. As she gathered up her things to leave, the MacKenzie-crest needlework slid off the table. Uncle Mac picked it up.

"'*Lucero non uro,*'" he said in surprise "That's my family crest. Do you know what our motto means?"

"I think it's 'I shine, not burn.'"

"Exactly," Uncle Mac said, looking impressed. He paused and then said with a smile, "Do you mind if I ask who this is for?"

"It's for Paul." Sierra felt a little awkward. Did Uncle Mac have any idea Sierra was dating his nephew through the mail?

"Really." It was a statement, not a question. He looked as if he were processing the information, trying to decide what he thought of this connection between the two of them. A gentle grin came across his face. "For any special occasion?"

"For Christmas," Sierra said, carefully putting the needlework in her backpack. "If I get it done, that is. It's taking a lot longer than I thought."

"Ah, but therein lies the value," Uncle Mac said, walking her to her car. "All things that hold lasting value in our lives take a long time to work on. Even relationships. Especially relationships."

As Uncle Mac opened her door, Sierra knew he was trying to convey some message to her. She wanted to tell him this relationship wasn't one-sided. Paul wrote to her all the time, and he was as committed to their relationship as she was. But that kind of validation probably needed to come from Paul, not from Sierra. She decided not to say anything in her own defense. Instead, she would mention it to Paul and let him enlighten his own uncle.

Just before Uncle Mac shut Sierra's car door, he smiled at her and said, "Thanks for your help tonight. You did fine. If I could give you any words of wisdom, I'd encourage you to think of 1 Corinthians 13."

"The love chapter?" Sierra asked. She had expected him to say, "Go home and read your counseling manual again so you'll be better prepared."

"Yes, the love chapter. What's the first characteristic listed?"

Sierra thought quickly. " 'Love is patient'?"

"Exactly. 'Love is patient.' There, that's my word of wisdom for you." He closed her door and waved.

Sierra drove the short distance home trying to decipher Uncle Mac's message. Was he saying she needed to be patient with herself as she learned how to do this counseling? That she needed to be patient with the people who called in? Or was he trying to protect his nephew by telling her that if she truly loved Paul she would be patient?

" 'Love is patient,' " Sierra repeated aloud as she parked the car in front of her house. "I can be patient."

chapter nine

"How was your weekend?" Randy asked Sierra on Monday morning. He leaned against her locker, greeting her with his usual cheerfulness and crooked grin.

"Well, let's see," Sierra said. "Our house caught on fire on Thanksgiving Day, my sister is mad at me, and last night on the Highland House hot line, I think I did permanent damage to every single person I talked to. I guess it was a good weekend. How was yours?"

"Your house caught on fire?" Randy said, extracting the crisis that most intrigued him.

"While my dad was praying, the marshmallows on top of the sweet potatoes caught on fire and ruined the oven and the cabinets above it. The house still smells awful. We're supposed to get the new oven tomorrow."

"Did the fire engine come?"

"Yes, the fire engine came."

"Cool."

Sierra shook her head at her take-everything-in-stride

buddy. "It was not my favorite Thanksgiving. How was yours?"

"Boring compared with yours."

"Hey, I heard from Vicki that your band is going to play at The Beet next Friday. That's great, Randy!"

He nodded, not appearing overly impressed with his own success. The Beet was a nightclub for teens in downtown Portland that offered music and nonalcoholic beverages on the weekends. Randy and his band had been together for only few months, but they had worked long, hard hours to get their sound just right. A gig at The Beet represented a breakthrough.

"Now here's the big question," Sierra said, slamming her locker shut as the bell rang. "What are you guys going to call yourselves?"

"We've narrowed it down," Randy said. "It's either The Smarties or The Slaymeyets."

"Where did that one come from?"

"The book of Job where he says, 'Though he slay me, yet will I hope in him.' Get it? Slay-me-yet."

"It sounds like Slimey-ettes."

"I know. That's the problem."

"So you have to come up with a name by Friday."

"Basically, yeah."

Sierra and Randy entered their first-period class. He put his arm around her and gave her shoulder a friendly squeeze. "All suggestions from friends will be cheerfully considered."

Sierra laughed. "Okay. I'll get serious about thinking up a name for you guys now that you're practically employed and everything. They are going to pay you for Friday night, aren't they?"

Randy shrugged. "We didn't ask."

As Sierra slid into her seat, a few possible names came to mind, such as "The Broke Boys" or "The Moths in the Pocket." For fun she jotted them down, just to see if they sparked other thoughts.

By lunchtime Sierra's list contained 17 names. She read them off to her friends, who had gathered at Lotsa Tacos for a quick, off-campus lunch.

"How about The Moths?" Tre asked as Sierra went down her list. Tre was from Cambodia, and Sierra often wondered what he thought when his friends became loud and rowdy, since his nature was to be reserved.

"That doesn't give a pretty image," Vicki said. She sipped her diet soda and scrunched up her petite nose. Vicki was gorgeous, in Sierra's opinion. As a matter of fact, Vicki was everything Sierra thought she was not. Vicki's green eyes and silky brown hair complemented her delicate features and smooth skin. Whenever Sierra looked at Vicki, Sierra wished she didn't have freckles and that a swish of a mascara wand would do to her eyes what it did to Vicki's. Paul had said when he first met Sierra that he liked her not wearing makeup.

The whisper of a memory of Paul made Sierra swallow. She wondered if anyone noticed the way a smile crept up her face and refused to leave. She wished Paul were here now, with her buddies. He would like them. He would have great comments to make. He might even have the perfect name for the group on the tip of his tongue.

"The Moths," Randy repeated, trying to decide if he liked it. "Maybe. You know, moths are drawn to light, and we're drawn to God's light."

"Yeah, but moths flock to the light bulb and then get fried," Vicki pointed out. "Not a real spiritual image there. How about the Light Bulbs? You know, like when a cartoon character gets a good idea and a light bulb appears over his head? You could have a cute logo."

"That's what we need," said Warner with a huff. "A cute logo." He was the band's very tall bass player and Sierra's least favorite member of the group. Warner was always putting his arm around Sierra, and she couldn't get him to understand that she didn't like it. She appreciated Randy putting his arm around her because they were buddies. But when Warner did it, he seemed to place so much weight on her that she felt smothered. Plus he would never let go on his own. He kept his arm around her as if he hoped people would think they were together.

"You know, we could abbreviate it," Randy suggested. "What do you think of The LB's?"

"It makes me think of boarding school in Peru," Margo said. She was a missionary kid who had started at Royal Academy a few months ago, when her family had come home on furlough. She had been hanging around with their gang for several weeks. "When we did reports for Bible class, they used to say, 'Make sure to make a note if you use the LB.'"

"What's that?" Tre asked.

"The Living Bible. It's a modern paraphrase of the

Bible, and we had tons of them in the library at school," Margo said.

"I like The LB's," Vicki said.

"Could have double meaning," Sierra suggested. "You know that old saying about how we're the only Bible some people may ever read, so we're like walking, living, breathing Bibles."

"And lights," Randy added. "We're supposed to be lights in the darkness. That's our band's purpose. I like the name. What do you guys think?"

Tre nodded. Warner gave a stoop-shouldered shrug.

"I think it's great!" Vicki said.

Margo glanced at her watch. "I think we'd better get back, or we'll be late again and end up sitting around in detention on Friday."

"You didn't say what you thought of the name The LB's," Warner said to Sierra as they left Lotsa Tacos. He plopped his thick arm across her shoulder, and she felt the same weight inside that she felt across her back.

Grabbing his wrist and removing his arm, Sierra said, "I like the name. I don't like it when you lean on me like that."

Warner looked surprised. Sierra didn't think he should be, since she had told him the same thing before. This time she wanted to make sure he got the message.

"Look, Warner, I mean it when I say I don't want you to put your arm around me anymore. Okay?"

"I'm just being friendly," he said defensively.

The others climbed inside Vicki's car. But Sierra wasn't through making her point.

"It doesn't feel friendly to me. It feels uncomfortable, and I don't want you to do it. Okay? Just don't put your arm around me anymore. Got it?"

Warner shrugged his agreement. He folded his tall frame into the front seat of Vicki's car. Sierra climbed into the back with Margo. No one spoke as they drove the few blocks back to school.

Just before they pulled into the school parking lot, Warner turned around and said, "Do you have a boyfriend, Sierra?"

Without hesitating, she said, "Yes, as a matter of fact, I do."

Vicki stared at her with large eyes, as if she thought Sierra were telling a lie.

"He's in Scotland right now," Sierra filled in for Vicki's benefit as well as Margo's and Warner's. "His name is Paul. Why do you ask?"

Appearing satisfied with her answer, Warner said, "I thought something was going on this past month. You haven't come to watch us practice or hang out with Randy the way you used to. Since you weren't interested in Randy, I thought maybe the rest of us losers might have a chance."

His comment produced a more sympathetic response from Margo than from Vicki or Sierra. "You're not a loser, Warner. Don't talk like that," Margo said.

Vicki parked the car and walked close to Sierra while Warner and Margo took their time.

"Would I be correct in assuming a few things are going on in your life that I haven't heard about?" Vicki said in a low voice.

"You mean about Paul?"

"Of course about Paul. Or did you just say that to get Warner to leave you alone? Because if you did, I wouldn't blame you. He kept following me around last year and drove me crazy."

Vicki and Sierra had to part ways to go to their separate classes. They were already late, so Vicki added, "Wait for me here after class."

Sierra did wait afterward, but when Vicki didn't show up after a few minutes, Sierra hurried to her next class. One tardy a day was more than enough. The pair didn't catch up with each other until after school in the parking lot.

"Do you want to go shopping with me?" Sierra asked. "I need to run by Wrinkle in Time to look for something to wear for my picture for Paul."

"Is this the picture I'm supposed to take of you when the rain stops?" Vicki asked.

Sierra nodded.

Vicki looked up at the billowy clouds that seemed to herald clear skies. "We could take it today."

"I couldn't find anything to wear, so I thought if I could buy something at Wrinkle in Time, I'd feel a lot better about the picture."

"I have time," Vicki said. "Do you want to drive or should I? I have to be home by 5:00."

"Let's take both cars."

"On one condition," Vicki said. "When we get there, you have to tell me absolutely everything about Paul. Every single detail that I somehow was not informed of, like, for instance, when you two actually became a couple."

Sierra nodded. She had a 20-minute drive alone in which to find a way to explain her relationship with Paul to Vicki. That wouldn't be so hard if only she knew how to define it herself. Was he truly her boyfriend? What if he were still living in Portland? Yes, she was certain they would be dating. Wasn't it the same now even though the miles separated them?

Sierra coaxed her '79 Rabbit out of the school parking lot and into the three o'clock flow of traffic with Vicki right behind her.

Yes, she convinced herself, it was the same. Paul was her boyfriend.

chapter ten

SIERRA AND VICKI ARRIVED AT THE SMALL VINTAGE clothing shop at the same time. As soon as Vicki exited her car, she began to pepper Sierra with questions about Paul.

Sierra heard herself say, "We're dating by mail. We write each other almost every day. I just sent him a four-page letter."

Vicki looked delighted. "I knew he sent you a picture for your birthday, but I had no idea you two were this far along in your relationship. It's great, Sierra. You know I think he's wonderful, handsome, and even a little mysterious."

Vicki had met Paul at the Highland House last spring. At that time, Sierra thought Vicki was interested in him. But as far as Sierra could tell, Paul had never showered Vicki with the kind of attention she was after. Sierra was surprised, since Vicki was the center of attention in most of the circles in which she orbited. Now Sierra was glad Vicki knew Paul and thought he was wonderful. Sierra felt it confirmed that she hadn't made all this up.

"Now can I tell you something?" Vicki said.

"Of course." Sierra felt a little shiver of concern that Vicki was going to say she had a secret crush on Paul and was jealous of Sierra. That's what had happened in the spring between Sierra and Amy, who had been Sierra's good friend at the time. Amy had a crush on Drake, and then, out of the blue, Drake had asked Sierra out. It caused a lot of tension even though Amy said at the time that she didn't mind. Now Amy and Sierra had little contact, since Amy was at a different school and was wrapped up in her boyfriend, Nathan. The strange thing was, Amy and Vicki had been good friends the year before and had a similar sort of rift in their friendship when they both liked the same guy. Sierra was enjoying Vicki's friendship and hoped that what Vicki was about to say would have nothing to do with guys.

"Remember?" Sierra joked. "I'm a certified hot-line adviser. You can tell me anything."

As they opened the door to enter the quaint little shop, Vicki smiled and said, "I think Randy and I might be getting together finally."

Sierra hadn't expected this news. "Really?" In her mind, she went over the last few times she had seen Randy and Vicki together. She hadn't been aware of a dating relationship blossoming between them.

Vicki nodded and smiled. "You know I've liked him for over a year."

"You have?" Sierra was still trying to process all this. She knew Vicki had invited Randy to a formal dinner in the spring and that lately Vicki had been hanging out with the band, but Vicki hadn't said anything about her interest in Randy.

"Of course I have. I thought it was obvious. But all along I thought Randy was interested in you, and only you, from here to eternity. So, not that I'm really humble or anything, but I was waiting to see what was going to happen with you and Randy. And now that you're going with Paul, I finally feel as though we can talk about Randy and me."

Sierra stood in the doorway, staring at Vicki. "This is all news to me."

"Good." Vicki slipped off her jacket in the warm shop and gave Sierra a contented smile. "I didn't want to get in the way if there was a chance of something happening between you and Randy."

Sierra assured Vicki, "Randy and I have been through this evaluation before. We're just buddies. I thought you knew that."

"Who knows anything for sure with relationships? All I know is that if it's time for something to happen between Randy and me, I'm ready for it. Your going with Paul makes things nice and uncomplicated."

The curtain to the changing room next to where Sierra and Vicki stood opened, and the customer, who couldn't have helped but hear their conversation, stepped out.

"Amy?" Sierra said. Sierra and Amy used to come to the Wrinkle in Time often, since they both loved vintage clothes, but they hadn't seen each other for several months. Amy's long, wavy, black hair was now cut short, with bangs that hung to the tips of her eyelashes and fluttered every time she blinked.

"Amy!" Vicki went up to her and offered a hug. "I've been hoping to see you. Did you get my phone messages about a month ago? I wanted to talk to you."

Amy didn't respond. Sierra had seen her this way before. Amy would clam up in situations that would cause Sierra to be wildly vocal.

Vicki plunged on. "I've been trying to call you because I wanted to tell you something. I went to camp this summer and got my life back on track with the Lord. I've asked several people to forgive me for stuff I did, and I wanted to apologize to you for what happened last year. You know, that big fight we had. I was wrong. I'm sorry, Amy."

Amy looked shocked. For a moment she didn't move. Then she said, "I'm sorry, too. I'm sorry everything went the way it did with us."

Vicki offered Amy another hug, which Amy hesitantly returned. "Thanks, Amy. I hope we can start over."

"We can start over. If that's what you want."

"That's definitely what I want!"

Sierra felt as if she should step in and ask forgiveness for something or offer a hug, too. She and Amy had talked heart-to-heart a few months before, but they hadn't exactly become friends again.

"It's so good to see you," was all Sierra could think to say.

Amy gave Sierra a quizzical look. "So you and Paul are together?"

Sierra nodded.

"When did he come back from Scotland?"

"He's still there. We write each other every day almost."

Amy smiled. "That's great. I'm happy for you. He's writing you every day?"

Sierra nodded, feeling herself blush a little. "Just about every day. I write him every day. You can get to know a lot about a person through letters."

"And the distance solves the purity problem, doesn't it?" Amy tilted her head and gave Sierra a knowing look.

The two of them had heatedly discussed physical intimacy when Amy confided how she and her boyfriend were getting involved. Sierra had come down hard on Amy, pushing Scripture verses at her and telling her how she needed to remain a virgin.

Vicki touched the ends of Amy's short hair. "I love this. When did you cut it?"

"A few weeks ago. Don't try it, either of you. You'll be sorry afterward."

"Are you going to buy that?" Vicki said, pointing at a blouse Amy had draped over her arm.

"No. It didn't fit. You want to try it on?"

"Yes, it's adorable," Vicki said. "Are you looking for blouses?"

Amy shook her head. "Just looking around. Killing some time."

"Then you can help us find the perfect outfit for Sierra. She's going to send Paul her picture for Christmas, and she needs something original."

Amy, who had always been enthusiastic on her shopping sprees with Sierra, took on a happier look. "Did you see those hats with the rolled brims over there?" She went over to a large wicker basket that sat on an old trunk and pulled out a soft, black hat. "Try this on," she said, placing it on Sierra's head.

"That's so cute on you," Vicki said.

"It looks like a Sierra hat," Amy agreed.

Sierra gave her reflection in the oak cheval glass a quick glance. "I don't necessarily want to look like me in the picture. I mean, look the way I always look."

Amy and Vicki exchanged confused glances.

"I want to look like me, only better. Does that make sense?"

"Ah!" Amy said knowingly.

"I saw just the dress." Vicki dashed over to the display in the front window. Without asking the store clerk, she reached into the display and lifted an emerald green, crushed-velvet dress from the peg where it hung on the side of the display.

"Just picture yourself in this," Vicki said, holding the dress up with a dramatic flare, as if she were the keeper of a fine Parisian dress shop. "In this dress, you will most definitely be transformed into the Sierra you long to be."

Sierra laughed.

"Go ahead," Amy urged. "Try it on."

"Are you guys sure?" Sierra asked, eyeing the short, green dress. It wasn't like anything she had ever worn before.

Vicki held it up to Sierra and said, "Look, it's going to be a perfect fit."

"Perfect," Amy echoed.

Sierra took the dress from Vicki with a tilt of her head and slipped into the dressing room. It felt strange yet natural that the three of them should be shopping like this. What felt good was that their long-standing disagreements and conflicts appeared to be cleared up. They could be friends and have fun together. But it was all so unexpected that Sierra felt surprised, too.

"Ta-da!" she announced, stepping out of the dressing room wearing the long-sleeved, scooped-neck dress. The dress was cut well. Sierra felt regal, elegant, and dressy as she smoothed her hands over the velvety curves of her frame.

"That's darling!" Vicki exclaimed.

"When did you get a figure?" Amy blurted out.

Sierra blushed. She had noticed her body making subtle changes over the summer, adding some gentle curves and rounding out in all the right places. It was embarrassing, though, to be 17 and just beginning to have the kind of figure all her friends started to acquire when they were much younger. During most of high school, she had suffered the silent agony of a late bloomer.

"Sierra, you look five years older in that dress," Amy said. "I can't believe how different it makes you look. You're gorgeous!"

"You think?" Sierra stood with her shoulders straight, taking in a full view of herself in the mirror. She couldn't stop smiling. She liked the way this dress and the attention of her friends made her feel. She didn't think of herself as the freckle-faced little tomboy dressed in baggy jeans, or the free spirit who wore long, gauze skirts. She felt like, well, like a young woman worthy of the honor of being called Paul's girlfriend. If she sent Paul a picture of herself in this dress, he would definitely notice how much she had matured. And if he harbored any doubts about Sierra's being old enough and mature enough to enter into a serious relationship, the sight of her in this green velvet dress would dissolve any such thoughts.

"I don't even want to know how much it costs," Sierra said to her friends, turning slightly and examining her backside in the full-length mirror. "I have to have this dress."

chapter eleven

HE THREE REUNITED FRIENDS EACH BOUGHT SOME-
thing at Wrinkle in Time. Sierra purchased the
dress and had enough money for the black hat,
which she thought would come in handy with all the rain
they had been having lately. Amy bought a small leather
purse with a long shoulder strap, and Vicki bought the
blouse Amy had been trying on when they entered the
shop.

They were enjoying their time together so much that
Vicki suggested they troop down the street to Mama Bear's
to celebrate becoming friends again. The welcoming fragrance of cinnamon invited them to enter the store and
find a quiet table.

Sierra felt content. She and her friends were nestled in
a cozy corner. She was enjoying a hot cup of tea, and the
new emerald green dress was in a shopping bag in her car.
All that was missing was Paul. She wished it were possible
for him to step through the door and physically enter into
her life. The best she could do was write another long letter
tonight and tell him everything—everything, that is, except

about the green dress. He would have to be surprised when he saw the picture of her wearing it. It was a delicious thought.

"What shoes are you going to wear with that dress?" Vicki asked. "It won't exactly go with your cowboy boots."

"Oh, you don't think so?" Sierra pretended her response was serious.

Amy chuckled. "You still have those disgusting boots? I thought they would have gotten up and walked away on their own by now."

"I love those boots," Sierra said with a pout.

"We know!" Amy and Vicki responded in unison.

They all laughed and picked at a shared cinnamon roll in the center of the table.

"So," Amy said, turning to Vicki, "you and Randy might be the latest couple around Royal?"

Vicki smiled. "Maybe. You never know. He cut his hair real short. Did you hear about that?"

Amy shook her head. "I don't hear much from anybody at Royal."

"He stopped a riot over the school dress code almost single-handedly," Vicki said. "He's my hero."

Sierra and Amy laughed.

"You and Randy," Amy said, shaking her head. "Is it 'senioritis' or what? Everyone is ending up with someone I'd never expect them to be interested in." Amy talked about some people Vicki knew who had gotten together, but Sierra didn't know them.

"How are you and Nathan doing?" Vicki asked. "How

long have you guys been together, six months now or seven?"

Amy swished the last sip of latte around in her cup. Without looking up, she said, "We broke up."

Sierra felt a squeeze in her heart. She never had wanted Amy to become involved with Nathan, but that didn't matter now. What mattered was that her friend had had her heart broken, and Sierra ached for her.

"Oh, Amy, I'm so sorry," Sierra said.

"You are?" Amy looked up, surprised.

"Yes, of course. It hurts, I'm sure, to break up after being together so long."

Amy looked down. "Yes. It hurts."

"What happened?" Vicki looked at Sierra and then at Amy. "I mean, if you don't mind my asking. I'm not trying to pry or anything."

Amy was silent for a moment. Then she looked up at Vicki. "We were doing fine for a long time. He's a great guy. He was there for me when my parents started their divorce."

"I heard about that," Vicki said. "I'm sorry. I should have been there for you, too. All those stupid arguments we had that we never resolved. I look back now, and I think it was so immature and pointless. I hurt a valuable friendship by not coming to you and trying to clear things up."

Amy drank her last sip of latte. "Well, it doesn't matter now. We're all back to being friends, and I'm glad for that. When I really needed someone, Nathan was there for me, and I'll probably always love him for that." She looked off into the distance as if pulling back a memory that she had sent far away.

"You don't have to tell us anything, if you don't want to," Sierra said.

"Yes she does," Vicki said, flashing her bright smile at Sierra and Amy. "We want to hear every gory detail."

Vicki's joking tone lightened the mood as all three of them chuckled. Then Sierra and Vicki sat silently, waiting for Amy to continue.

"I guess I was too demanding. That's what he said. I kind of lost my life and became wrapped up in his. We started to fight, which we never did the first few months. Then I found out he had lied to me about something. It wasn't a big thing. He told me he was going to stay home one night, but I found out he went to the movies with a bunch of other people, and I got mad. He said he just wanted a break from me. We didn't talk to each other for about a week, and then we got back together at work that weekend. We did okay for about another week and a half, and then it started all over again. We broke up for good about two weeks ago. He's already going out with someone else."

"That's awful," Sierra said.

"I thought you would say that that's what you had been praying for, that we would break up," Amy said. "Or at least I thought you would want to give me a good 'I told you so.'"

Sierra shook her head. "That's the last thing I want to give you, Amy. What I want to give you is my friendship. From my track record, I obviously don't know a lot about friendship, but one thing I do know is when a friend hurts, the other person hurts, too."

Amy turned misty-eyed and said, "Thanks, Sierra."

"Is there something wrong with me?" Vicki said. "I mean, I'm sorry, Amy, but I'm glad you broke up with Nathan. I'll admit it even if Sierra won't. I don't think he was the best guy in the world for you. Good riddance, I say."

"Vicki!" Sierra said.

Amy was quiet for a moment and then said, "So, Vicki, could you tell me how you really feel?"

The three of them laughed.

"I never have been one to hide my opinions," Vicki said.

"So I remember," Amy said. She quickly added, "I guess that's one of the things I always liked about both of you." She took in Sierra with her gaze before looking back at Vicki. "Both of you are strong, and I have to admit, I'm feeling pretty weak right now."

Sierra and Vicki gave Amy sympathetic looks.

"It's okay," Sierra said.

Amy shook her head. "You're both right, you know. He probably wasn't the best guy in the world for me. I guess it's a good thing we broke up when we did. And it's humbling for me to have to admit this, but I need you both to be my friends. I need you to hurt for me a little, like Sierra said. I think the worst part of the breakup was when I realized Nathan had friends to go to the movies with, and I didn't have anybody I could call. I had cut off all my friends from Royal Academy, and I hadn't even tried to make friends at my new school. I don't want to be lonely like that again."

Sierra reached over and gave Amy's wrist a squeeze. "You don't have to feel like that anymore. The three of us need to start doing stuff together again. I think God set it up for us to run into each other just so we could restart our friendship."

"Why don't we plan to meet here every Monday afternoon?" Vicki suggested.

"Agreed," Amy said. "As long as you'll both promise me one thing."

"What's that?" Sierra asked.

"Don't push the God stuff on me. I know what you guys believe, and I think it's great, Vicki, that you got your life back together with God this summer and everything, but don't put that stuff on me."

Neither Sierra nor Vicki answered.

"Promise me," Amy said.

"I can't promise I won't talk about God," Sierra said.

"Me either," Vicki said. "He's the biggest thing in my life."

"Okay," Amy said, holding up her hands. "You can talk about all that God stuff, but don't expect me to participate, okay?"

Sierra and Vicki nodded.

"So what time should we meet on Mondays?" Vicki asked. She glanced up at the bear-shaped clock on the wall; the clock face was in the bear's tummy. "Oh, no!" she cried. "I was supposed to be home at 5:00, and it's already 5:30. Is there a phone here?"

Sierra led Vicki to the phone in the back of the bakery and asked Mrs. Kraus, who was in the kitchen, if it was okay for Vicki to make a local call. Sierra left Vicki there and returned to the table, where Amy sat alone, folding the ends of her napkin in tidy triangles.

"I need to get going, too," Sierra said. "Before I forget, Randy's band is playing at The Beet this Friday. Do you want to go with us or meet us there? He would love to have as many friendly faces in the audience as possible."

"Sure. I'll just meet you guys there. Nathan and I used to go to The Beet when we were first dating, but I doubt he'll be there. If he shows up with his new girlfriend, you'll keep me from scratching her eyes out, won't you?"

Sierra knew Amy well enough to realize her hot-tempered friend was more serious than kidding. "I'll be there for you, Amy. I said that a couple of months ago, but now it looks as if I'll have a chance to prove it. Yes, I'll be there for you, even if I have to cut all your fingernails before we go inside."

"Already did that," Amy said, holding up both hands and showing her nibbled-off nails. "When Nathan and I broke up, I cut my hair, cut my nails, and cut up a picture of the two of us at the Portland Jazz Festival. Am I pathetic or what?"

"You're not pathetic."

Amy met Sierra's comforting gaze. "Thanks, Sierra. I only hope I can be as encouraging to you one day when Paul breaks your heart."

Sierra felt her lips part, but no words tumbled out. Vicki rushed up to the table and announced that she had to fly. The three of them went their separate ways with plans to meet at The Beet on Friday night.

Sierra hurried home, eager to try on her new dress again, but even more eager to check for a letter from Paul. The mailbox was empty, so she headed for the kitchen and asked her mom, who was busy admiring the new oven that had been installed that afternoon, whether they had gotten any mail. Mrs. Jensen told Sierra there had been none for her.

Retreating to her room, Sierra thought of Amy's final statement about Paul breaking Sierra's heart. She always felt a little insecure when she didn't hear from Paul for a few days, but then a letter or postcard would arrive, and her fears would dissolve. She wished she had said something to Amy about not needing to plan on comforting Sierra because Paul was not going to break her heart.

Was he?

She flopped onto her unmade bed and took Paul's picture from her nightstand. She visually retraced every detail of his face. This was not the face of a guy who was out to break her heart. But then Nathan certainly hadn't intended to break Amy's heart, had he? Nobody ever sets out with that as the goal of the relationship. It just happens. Things change. People change.

Sierra rolled onto her side and held Paul's picture close. She couldn't change her feelings for him—ever. She wouldn't. And he wouldn't change, either. They would only grow closer and closer. Then he would come back from Scotland, and . . . What if he didn't come back from Scotland? What if he stayed another year or three or 50?

Sierra pursed her lips together and thought hard. Why did she have to go to a college in the States next fall? Why couldn't she go to the same university Paul was attending in Edinburgh?

She sat up, her mind flooding with plans. She could go over to Scotland as soon as school was out and find a job somewhere doing something. She could take a train down to Switzerland for a week and visit Christy so Paul wouldn't grow tired of her the way Nathan had gotten tired of Amy. She would have her own friends there, too, so she wouldn't smother Paul. But they would be close. They would study together, and on weekends he would take her hiking in the Highlands and out to his grandmother's cottage for tea on Sunday afternoons.

Sierra hopped up and began to pace the floor. She needed to find the address for admissions and send in an application right away. Should she tell Paul or wait until she heard back from the university? Her parents would need to know, of course. But if Tawni could announce she was going off to Reno, why couldn't Sierra announce she was going to Edinburgh?

Scooping up the new green dress, Sierra held it in front of her and waltzed around the clutter on her floor. Never before had her spirit soared to such dizzying heights. She laughed when she thought how she would show everyone what a magnificent free spirit she was. She could just picture herself, the minute she had her high school diploma in hand, taking the next plane to Scotland.

chapter twelve

"**N**O," M**R**. J**ENSEN** **SAID FIRMLY**. H**E SAT IN HIS**
desk chair, showing by his crossed arms
that he wasn't going to budge.

"But, Dad, can we at least talk about it?"

"You're not thinking clearly right now, Sierra," her
father said.

Sierra shifted uncomfortably in her favorite chair in the
study. She had on her new green dress, which she had
worn to dinner for effect. She got effect, all right. Her
parents said more than once they were startled by her
choice, that the dress was so unlike her other clothes. Their
less-than-favorable response didn't dampen her spirits
when it came to her plans for school in Scotland. She did
decide to wait until after dinner when her mom was helping Dillon and Gavin with their homework before she
talked to her dad in the study. When he closed the door
behind them, Sierra had excitedly blurted out her plan.

That's when her father said no.

"I am too thinking clearly," Sierra protested. "This is
something I'd love to do. My grades are good enough; you

know that. I've been to Europe twice before. Why can't I go to school there?"

"Sierra," her dad said, unfolding his arms and leaning forward, "you know nothing about this university. Your only reasons for going there would be adventure and, if I can venture a guess, to be close to Paul. Those are not good reasons for selecting a college. Financially, we're depending on several scholarships to come through for you. I know nothing about how scholarships might transfer to Edinburgh."

"We can find out," Sierra said. "We can ask. I'll ask. I'll research it."

Her dad shook his head. "The answer will still be no."

"Why?" Sierra pleaded. "You let Tawni take off to California, where she lives near her boyfriend."

"That's different. Tawni started to date Jeremy after she moved to San Diego; she didn't move there to be near him. And Tawni is 19, almost 20. You just turned 17 a few weeks ago."

Sierra let out a frustrated sigh. She knew her parents had a thing about the magical age of 18. Her two older brothers and older sister had all stayed home until they were 18, and then they were given several options of how their mom and dad would help them get on their feet. Sierra knew that to leave home before she was 18 would be the same as cutting herself off from the family blessing.

"Sierra, what I'm most concerned about is what's gotten into you."

"What do you mean?"

"This dress, for one thing. It's so unlike you. And where

did the idea you wanted to be near Paul come from?"

"We've been writing each other almost every day. It's just that I'm the one who brings in the mail, so nobody knows how often he writes me. I write him all the time."

"Is that why you kept disappearing during Thanksgiving?"

"What do you mean?"

"You weren't around much. Were you going off to write Paul?"

"Yes. What's wrong with that?"

"Did you spend any time with your relatives?" her dad asked.

"Yes, I did."

"Without being told?"

"Well . . ." Sierra was hard-pressed to come up with a yes. She knew Aunt Frieda had been upset that Sierra had avoided Nicole and Molly, the two cousins who were close to her age. Frieda's parting words to Sierra had been sharp, but Sierra had brushed them off. Many of Frieda's words had little stingers attached to them. Sierra always figured that the only sure way to keep them from penetrating her skin was to brush them off quickly.

"You haven't been yourself lately," Mr. Jensen said.

Sierra considered saying she was in love, but she knew that would not score points with her dad. "I'm growing up, Dad; that's all. This is me—the new, improved me. I know I'm a late bloomer, and I'm experiencing at 17 what most girls experience much earlier." The words tumbled out before she had time to evaluate them. "But like it or not, I'm becoming a woman. No, I take that back. I am a woman. I'm not your little girl anymore."

Sierra had blurted out her opinions many times over the past 17 years. Sometimes she regretted being vocal. Sometimes she caught herself before she really blew it. Sometimes she thought about it later and was glad she had spoken up. Still other times she thought about it and wished she hadn't said anything.

Then there was this time. It was like no other. With her words, she had just cut an invisible string that had tied her heart to her father's for all these years. She was making it clear she wanted to take the end of that severed string and tie it to Paul's heart.

And her father was telling her no.

"We need to talk some more," Mr. Jensen said after a long moment of silence. "This isn't a good time. But we need to talk some more."

"Okay," Sierra said calmly. She set as her goal to prove to her dad she was composed and mature and could discuss whatever he felt was necessary to talk through. "Let me know when it's convenient for you."

"I will." Her dad left her alone in the study, sitting stiffly in her favorite chair with her short green dress and her pounding heart.

The next day Sierra raced home from school, certain a letter from Paul would be waiting for her, and there was. The letter was short, but every word tasted sweet as she stopped in her tracks on the front porch to read it:

A quick note, Sierra. I'm swamped with exams, and unlike you, I can't boast a 4.0. So I must torture my

*brain beyond its natural limits. I'm glad you liked the
photo. It was taken in one of my favorite hiking areas.
I hope to go there this weekend, if the storms let up. It's
been nothing but rain here for days. You asked about
my birthday. It's December 10, and if I may be so bold
as to make a birthday wish, I'm hoping for a picture of
you to put here on my writing desk. Your breezy smile
during the long hours of study will ease my pain. Must
fly.*

> *With all good wishes to you,*
> *Paul*

Sierra quickly calculated backward from December 10.
If she had the picture taken this afternoon, she could run
it over to the one-hour photo lab, find a frame, wrap it,
and mail it tomorrow. That would give it a week and a half
to arrive. It was close.

"Mom?" Sierra called out as she entered the house.
"Mom, where are you?" She searched until she found her
mother stretched out on the couch with a blanket over her.
"Oh, are you okay?"

"Just feeling tired. What is it?"

"I need a favor. Could you take some pictures of me?
It's not raining for once, and I wanted some photos taken
in the backyard. I have the film and everything."

"Do you need it done this instant?" Mrs. Jensen didn't
look as if she wanted to move from her cozy spot.

"No, that's okay. Sorry I woke you up. We can do it
later."

But Sierra didn't want to do it later. She wanted it done
now. Heading for the kitchen, she tried Vicki's number.

No answer. She called Randy, but his mom said he wasn't home yet. Going through the list, she called other people she knew. No one was available. She phoned Vicki again. Still no answer. Desperate, Sierra was about to wake her mom. After all, it had been a whole five minutes since their conversation. But then Granna Mae shuffled into the kitchen.

"Hello, Lovey. How was your day?"

"Great! Hey Granna Mae, would you mind taking my picture in the backyard?"

Granna Mae's slowed reflexes caused her to give Sierra a funny stare before answering. "I suppose I could."

"Great. Wait here. I'll be right back."

Sierra blasted upstairs, changed into her green dress, applied a quick splash of makeup, and tried to corral her unruly hair.

"I'm coming," she called downstairs as she grabbed the camera and made sure the film she had loaded the other day was ready to roll.

"Okay, I'm all set," Sierra said, dashing into the kitchen.

But Granna Mae wasn't there. Not wanting to yell and wake up her mom, Sierra tried to quietly skitter around downstairs, searching for her grandmother. She went back upstairs and found Granna Mae in her room, quietly look-ing out the window.

"Okay, I'm ready," Sierra said. "Can you take my pic-ture now? In the backyard? I thought it would be pretty by the tree that hasn't lost all its leaves yet. The little, bright yellow one."

"All right," Granna Mae agreed.

She followed Sierra with slow, steady steps. By the time they were down the stairs and out the back door, Granna Mae was winded. It took her a few minutes before she was able to manage the camera.

"I'll be standing right here," Sierra said, going over to the tree with the yellow leaves. "And you take the shot from my knees up because I don't have any shoes to go with this dress." She stood there, barefooted, shivering slightly in the scoop-necked dress. "You know which button to push, don't you?"

"Say cheese!" Granna Mae said. She snapped the picture.

"Keep taking them," Sierra said. "We can use up the whole roll. Get some close-ups. I want this to be a nice picture."

She stood as straight as she could and smiled for the camera. As the shutter clicked again, Sierra thought of Paul's words, that her breezy smile would ease his study pains. He was such a poet. She smiled more broadly and hoped the glow in her eyes, the glow that burned there for Paul alone, would show up in the photos.

chapter thirteen

A FTER SIERRA COUNTED 24 SNAPS OF THE CAMERA, she thanked her grandmother and took back the camera. "It's cold out here," Sierra said. "You'd better get warmed up inside."

"All right," Granna Mae agreed. "I hope your pictures come out nicely, Emma."

Granna Mae had confused Sierra with Emma more than once. As the youngest of Granna Mae's children, Emma in her younger days had looked like Sierra.

Did Emma ever come home with a short green dress? Sierra wondered. *If so, what did her father say to her about it?*

Brutus barked wildly from the end of his chain as Sierra helped Granna Mae up the leaf-covered back steps.

"Sorry, Brutus," Sierra called over her shoulder, "you can't come back in the house until you've had a bath, and I don't have time to give you one now."

"Maybe he's hungry," Granna Mae suggested. "Or thirsty. Has anyone checked his water bowl lately?"

"I'll take a look," Sierra promised. "Let's just get you

back up to your room, where it's nice and toasty."

"I've enjoyed our little walk," Granna Mae said. "Let's do it again tomorrow."

"Okay," Sierra said. She held Granna Mae's elbow all the way up to her room, where the wearied woman sat down in her recliner.

"Thank you, dear. That was lovely."

Sierra gave Granna Mae a kiss on the cheek and then hurried to her own bedroom. She was cold, too, so she changed into her favorite pair of jeans and an old fisherman's knit sweater that used to be Wesley's. Her toes were icy. Pulling on a pair of socks, she shoved her feet into her cowboy boots. Then, because she remembered her dad's old saying about covering your head if you want to warm up fast, she reached for her new black hat with its rolled brim and popped it on her head. Her crazy blonde curls poured out from under the hat like party streamers.

Oh well, Sierra thought, catching a glimpse of herself in her mirror. *What I look like won't matter to the people at the one-hour photo shop.*

She hurried downstairs. Brutus's persistent barking stopped her.

"Okay, you big lug. I'm coming." Sierra went out the back door to check on him. Just as Granna Mae had suggested, he had neither water nor food.

"You poor baby," Sierra said, turning on the garden hose and pulling it closer so he could lap up the water as she rinsed out his water dish and filled it. "Can you wait an hour for your dinner? I'll be back then. If Gavin hasn't fed you yet, I promise I will."

Brutus stuck out his long, moist tongue and panted appreciatively.

"See you later, buddy." Sierra returned the water hose to the side of the yard and headed for the back steps. She smiled to herself, thinking how fun it was going to be to send her picture to Paul and wondering what his letter would say when he wrote to thank her for it.

She was on the second step when she heard her mother call her name. Sierra looked up, rosy-cheeked and smiling.

Click. Mrs. Jensen stood on the landing with the camera.

"I already have the pictures, Mom. There shouldn't be any film left."

Just then the camera began to automatically rewind.

"I guess there was one more," her mom said.

"I'm taking the film to the one-hour place. Is there anything you want me to pick up on the way home?"

"No, but thanks for asking. Are these pictures for a school project or something? Why the rush?"

"It's for Paul. I just found out his birthday is December 10, and I have to mail the photo off to him by tomorrow if it's going to arrive on time."

"I see," Mrs. Jensen said. She looked a little confused. Or was it concerned?

Sierra felt the need to explain. "He sent me a picture of himself for my birthday, remember? And now he's asked if I'd send him a picture of me for his birthday."

"I see," Mrs. Jensen said again.

But when Sierra looked more closely at her mother, she was afraid her mother didn't see at all. If her mom

understood what it was like to have a blossoming relationship with the most amazing guy on the planet, then she
would understand why this was all so important to Sierra.
But her mom didn't seem to understand.

"I'll be home in a little over an hour," Sierra said,
grabbing the camera and her backpack. "Love you. See you
later. Bye-bye!" She flew out the front door and hopped
into her car.

Only one clerk was working at the photo lab when
Sierra dropped off her film, but he guaranteed her it would
be ready in an hour. Deciding to use the time to find a
card, a frame, and maybe the ingredients for the tea party
for Paul's Christmas present, she hurried out of the shop.
She could send the tea party for his birthday, instead, if
she could find everything right away.

Her shopping spree took more than an hour, but she
managed to buy everything she was after. The only bad
part was that it cost more than she had figured, and she
only had enough money left for the pictures. The quarter
of a tank of gas in her car would have to last until the next
paycheck.

"There you are. I have a question about one of your
pictures," the photo clerk said when Sierra entered the
shop.

"Yes?" She began to fan through the stack of pictures.
One of them showed the tree in full length and only the
very top of Sierra's head. The next one was of her arm and
her torso. Another was just her face, but it was fuzzy. Sierra
groaned.

I bet he's going to ask how anyone could fail so miserably

*with an entire roll of film. Why did I ask Granna Mae to do
this, especially when I wasn't sure she was thinking clearly?
He's probably astounded I would admit to owning them.*

"We would like to buy one of your pictures," the clerk
said.

"You're kidding."

"No. We occasionally buy some of the really good shots
and put them up in the window to advertise."

"The really good shots?" Sierra repeated.

"This one," he said, pulling out a photo from the bottom of the stack.

It was the one her mom had taken. Sierra had to agree.
Everything was just right. The background was a smear of
gold and orange from the trees; Sierra was smiling expec-
tantly, and her cheeks were blushed, which made her eyes
sparkle. The picture was from her chest up, and the dark
felt hat with the rolled brim contrasted with the fire-
colored leaves behind her. But the best part was her hair.
The blonde curls fell in a gleeful cascade, lit by the late-
afternoon sun and giving off a golden shine that overshad-
owed the autumn leaves.

"Do you have any more like this?" the clerk asked.

"Nope. That was just the last frame, and it was sort of
taken by accident."

"It's a very good photo. May we buy it?"

"You can buy a copy, but I need this original, and I'll
need the negative."

"Good deal," he said. "If you'll sign a release form, the
company will mail you the check."

"Great. Thanks!"

Sierra felt kind of special as she told her news at the dinner table that night. She didn't show anyone the other pictures because she didn't want Granna Mae to know what a goofball job she had done.

"Did you find out how much they're going to pay you?" Mrs. Jensen asked.

"Only $20. Do you want me to split it with you since you were the photographer?"

"No, of course not. You probably need it for Christmas gifts."

Later that night, in her room, Sierra realized how true her mom's words were. She had depleted all her funds on the needlepoint kit, the film, the frame, and everything else for Paul. Now her money for gifts for her family was all gone. Sierra realized as she wrapped the picture that she didn't even have enough money to pay for the postage to mail the birthday box.

She didn't let that worry her, though. At least she had pulled together exactly what she wanted to give Paul. The card alone had cost $3, but it was a gorgeous illustration of a guy and a girl walking hand-in-hand through a meadow of wildflowers. Inside it said, "Thinking of you on your birthday and sending more wishes than your arms can hold." She liked that it was tender and a little bit mushy.

The tea-party items were what had depleted her account. She had bought a lot of little goodies, especially candies and treats she didn't remember being able to buy in England or Ireland when she was there almost a year ago. Paul was probably ready for some good ol' American candy by now. She also bought a small cake that came wrapped for school lunches and a package of birthday candles. She included a can of mixed nuts; a party-favor bag of horn blowers, noisemakers, and birthday hats; and a plastic pin-the-tail-on-the-donkey game. Sierra also bought a black ceramic mug to go with a little bag of gourmet coffee. The coffee fit inside the mug, and she wrapped it with bubble packaging before putting it in the birthday-party care package.

Several hours later, Sierra had prepared everything just the way she wanted it. She had debated a long time before she wrapped the framed picture and laid it carefully in the box. It wasn't that she didn't like the photo her mom had taken. It looked exactly like Sierra. That was the problem. The girl in the green dress would have made much more of an impression. But she was out of money and had no time to find someone to take another roll of pictures.

Sierra lined up all the poor shots Granna Mae had taken of her. She decided if she cut them up—an arm out of this one, a leg here, her head from this one, she could form a puzzle of herself. It made her wonder if Granna Mae viewed the world in that fragmented way some days. Sierra decided it might make an interesting art project to try to fit all the picture pieces together. Not tonight, though. The wrapping had taken a long time, and she still had homework to do.

At 10 minutes after midnight, when Sierra finished the letter that went with the surprise box, she was exhausted. Taping up the box and writing Paul's address on the front seemed to take a lot of effort. No way could she do any homework tonight. She would have to finish it tomorrow before class somehow.

The "somehow" didn't happen. The day zoomed by, and Sierra had to take a zero for one of her English assignments. She was mad. Now she would have to do extra-credit work so her grade wouldn't suffer. And the last thing she needed in her already busy schedule was more homework.

Sierra had borrowed $10 from her mom that morning so she could mail the gift. She drove to the post office right after school and then went to Mama Bear's Bakery to see if she could pick up some extra hours to earn more holiday money. Mrs. Kraus checked the schedule and offered Sierra two additional mornings during Christmas week, which Sierra agreed to take. It wouldn't help her current financial crisis, but if she had to borrow money, she needed to earn more to pay it back.

When she arrived at home, she immediately checked the mail. Nothing from Paul. She tried not to let it bother her. Still, a gloomy mist settled on her as she thought of how hard she had worked on his gift box the night before, even at the expense of taking a zero in English.

Sierra knew it would be difficult for her to finish her homework again tonight because she was so far behind on the needlepoint for Paul that she needed to put in several hours on it. Tomorrow she worked; Friday was the big night at The Beet; Saturday she worked again; Sunday was church; and Sunday night she volunteered at the Highland House. That didn't leave much time for putting tiny little stitches in a row.

Sierra hurried up to her room and went right to work on the needlepoint. Her thoughts were of Paul, and nothing but Paul.

As she carefully stitched the top flame on the mountain, she thought, *All I can say is, he had better appreciate everything I'm doing for him!*

chapter fourteen

"OVER HERE!" AMY CALLED TO SIERRA AND Vicki. Amy waved her arm and indicated they should join her at the corner table in The Beet. Waves of loud music and louder voices crashed over Sierra and Vicki as they threaded their way through the crowd.

"This place is packed!" Vicki exclaimed, as she pulled off her jacket and hung it over the back of the chair next to Amy. "I've never seen it so full."

"Yeah, well, guess who the main group is tonight?" Amy had to shout over the piped-in music. "The L's."

"You're kidding!" Vicki shouted back. "Here? At our little place?"

Sierra had heard The L's before and really liked the energetic sound of their trumpets and saxophones combined with guitars.

"So, The LB's have to open for The L's?" Vicki asked.

"Yes," Amy said. "Only our guys aren't The LB's anymore. They thought it sounded too wannabe, performing just before The L's and everything."

"What are they calling themselves?" Sierra asked. The loud music was beginning to hurt her ears.

Amy shrugged. "I think they're trying to decide right now."

Sierra settled into the straight-backed chair and moved closer to Amy. The table wobbled. Each of the chairs was a different style and painted a different color. Sierra liked the bold, crazy decor. A long, green canoe with a big hole in the bottom was suspended from the ceiling with a light hanging from the opening. A moose head hung over the stage area. The moose wore an oxygen mask on its long snout and a red flower over its right ear.

The admission into The Beet was $3 and a can of food, which was donated to the Salvation Army downtown. Sierra had a total of 37 cents to her name and had to borrow the $3 from Vicki to get in. Now a waitress dressed in green corduroy overalls stood by their table asking if they wanted to order something to drink. Sierra had to settle for water.

She pulled her needlepoint from her backpack, thinking she could add a few stitches while they waited for Randy's group to open the night's performance.

"What's that?" Amy asked.

"A gift I'm trying to finish for Christmas."

"Here?" Amy looked at Vicki and back at Sierra. "Hello, Sierra, this is not a quilting club. This is a night-club. You're supposed to talk, laugh, and have fun. Not sit and knit."

Sufficiently chided, Sierra returned the needlepoint to her backpack. "How can we talk? It's so loud."

"This isn't loud," Amy said. "Wait until the bands come out."

Sierra suddenly felt like an old lady. Since when did noise like this bother her? And why had she thought it would be a good idea to bring along a stitchery project? If she wasn't going to enter into the wacky atmosphere of this place, she might as well have stayed home.

Vicki waved at some friends of hers, and Amy looked around. "You guys don't see him, do you?"

"Who? Nathan?" Sierra asked.

"Of course Nathan. Tell me if you see him. I've been worrying about this all day. If he's here, I'm warning you, it could get ugly."

"You wouldn't do anything stupid," Vicki said confidently. She pulled her long, sleek hair back and wrapped it up in a scrunchie. "You have us here to support you. Is anyone else hot, or is it me?"

"It's hot in here," Sierra agreed.

She was about to suggest they go outside to cool off when the canned music stopped and a guy in a black stovepipe hat stepped onto the stage. "Dig that crazy beat!" His voice ricocheted off the walls and was answered by a chorus of regulars at The Beet, who gave their "code" response of "Time to move your feet!" Sierra had never seen anything like it. It was fun—silly, good, clean fun.

"Let's hear it for the Three-Two-Ones!"

"The Three-Two-Ones?" Sierra and Vicki echoed.

"They must have decided to try numbers instead of letters," Amy suggested, yelling over the roar of the applause.

Randy and the band hustled onto the stage, and the drummer immediately pounded out a steady rhythm. Sierra could tell Randy was nervous. Both sides of his mouth were turned up in a forced smile. When Randy normally smiled, it was a crooked half-grin. Tonight he looked a little like a kid at a spelling bee, standing tall and stiff with his feet pointed straight out and the guitar slung over his shoulder. He wore his black baseball cap with a ponytail attached to the back. At that moment, the moose in the oxygen mask over the stage appeared more natural than poor Randy.

The first song was one of Sierra's favorites. She thought the group played it flawlessly. The audience responded with wild applause, and Sierra began to breathe a little easier. At least the Three-Two-Ones were off to a good start, and they had the crowd with them. It would be hard not to have an enthusiastic response from this crowd, since everyone crammed into The Beet seemed to have come to have a good time.

Randy appeared to relax a bit on the second song and was smiling at Sierra with his usual crooked grin by the end of third song. Unfortunately, that song was also their last—and right when they were starting to crank.

"They were great!" Vicki said excitedly. "Didn't Randy look adorable?"

"He looked nervous," Sierra stated.

"At first, but then he loosened up."

After a short break, The L's were to come on. The server returned with the drinks, and Sierra gladly swigged her water. The crowded room was heating up. She wished she had worn a T-shirt instead of a sweater.

"Hey, Megan!" Vicki yelled at a girl across the room, who waved back.

Just then Amy grabbed Sierra's arm and pressed tightly. "There's Adam," Amy said. "He's Nathan's best friend. Is Nathan here? Have you seen him?"

Sierra looked over her shoulder. "No. He might not be here."

"If Adam's here, Nathan probably is. I don't want to see him."

"It's so crowded," Sierra said. "Even if he's here, you might not run into each other. I wouldn't worry about it if I were you."

"Well, you're not me," Amy snapped. "I'm going to leave. I'm not up to this."

"But The L's!" Sierra said.

Amy grabbed her purse and swung it over her shoulder. "I'll see you guys on Monday." She began to edge her way through the crowd.

Sierra and Vicki looked at each other.

"What is her deal?" Vicki said. "I don't get it."

"I'm going to go with her," Sierra heard herself say. She hadn't planned to make such a statement, but there it was. "Can you find a ride home?"

Vicki smiled. "Sure. I'll ask Randy."

Sierra grabbed her backpack and flashed a smile at Vicki, knowing that needing a ride from Randy was the best thing Vicki could think of happening to her tonight.

"I'll see you later," Sierra said.

Pushing her way through the thick crowd, Sierra tried

to see which way Amy had gone. The L's stepped onto the stage, and a lively blast of trumpet and sax opened the act. "If you give a man a fish . . . ," the lead singer began. Sierra wished she were staying. She liked this song; the music of the L's always had such a cheering effect on her. Instead, she was following her erratic friend, who had given no indication she wanted company.

Sierra stepped out into the cold night and spotted Amy along the side of the building. She was standing face-to-face with Nathan. In the glow of the large, red neon Beet sign over the entrance, Sierra could see the expression on Nathan's face. He did not look happy.

chapter fifteen

S IERRA DIDN'T KNOW WHAT TO DO. SHE STOOD ONLY
four feet away from Nathan and Amy, but Amy's
back was to her. Dozens of teens were milling
around the front of The Beet, and Sierra tried to blend in
so she wouldn't draw Nathan's attention. Would Amy be
mad if Sierra interrupted them? Should she just go back
inside? What if something bad happened? Amy had
sounded almost frightened about seeing Nathan. Might he
hurt her?

Sierra slung the backpack over her shoulder and shifted
her weight from one foot to the other. The night air cooled
her hot cheeks. She decided to move a little closer to hear
what was going on so she could determine if everything
was okay. Suddenly, Nathan reached over and took Amy
by the arm. Sierra couldn't tell if he was being rough
because she couldn't see Amy's face. All she knew was that
Amy wasn't pulling away. But what if Amy couldn't free
herself from his grasp?

Sierra decided she needed to jump in and defend her
friend. Wesley had taught her some self-defense tactics,

and Sierra had an air horn in her backpack. She quickly pulled it out, prepared to use it if necessary. The loud blast of noise, Wes had told her when he gave her the horn, would startle an attacker and give her enough time to run for safety.

Holding the air horn, Sierra carefully watched Nathan's every move. Amy put her head down, and Nathan grabbed her by the shoulders, looking as if he might start to shake her. Then he put his arm around her and hurried her toward the parking lot in back.

With her heart pounding, Sierra rushed after them, her finger poised on the air horn's trigger. When she was right behind them, she could tell Amy was crying. A burst of adrenaline gave Sierra the confidence she needed to point the air horn at the back of Nathan's head and press the trigger.

"Run, Amy, run!" Sierra screamed over the deafening blast.

Nathan dropped his arm from around Amy, covered his ears with his hands, and spun around to face Sierra. Sierra backed away, but Amy didn't move.

"Run, Amy, run!"

"Sierra!" Amy's tear-streaked face reflected shock. "What are you doing?"

"You were crying," Sierra stammered in the silence that now followed the loud blast. "He was forcing you to go with him."

"He was not," Amy said, now looking furiously at Sierra. "We were just going to talk things out."

"What is with you?" Nathan said, grabbing the air horn

away from Sierra. "What are you doing with this thing? And why are you following us?" Nathan wasn't a big guy, but he could look fierce when he wanted to—like now.

"I-I'm sorry. . . . I thought . . ."

"You thought what?" Amy said.

Sierra couldn't answer.

"You of all people should understand how important it is for friends to work out their unresolved issues." Amy had stopped crying. "Nathan and I need to talk, Sierra. We would like a little privacy to try to work a few things out here, if you don't mind."

"I-I'm sorry. . . ."

Nathan handed her the air horn. "Go rescue somebody who wants to be," he stated, giving Sierra a withering look. "Since that's apparently what you think your mission in life is."

Sierra apologized one more time and turned to go. Never had she felt so foolish. Here she thought she was helping her friend, but obviously Amy had a much stronger sense of loyalty to Nathan than she had let on. Swallowing hard, Sierra numbly stuffed the air horn into her backpack and made her way to the front door of The Beet.

"I already paid," she told the guy guarding the front door.

"I need to see your stub."

Sierra dug her hands into her pockets and then realized that Vicki had the stub, since she had paid for both of them. "My friend in there has it," she said.

The guy gave her a knowing nod. "Yeah, right. Sorry. No ticket, no laundry."

Sierra looked over his head into the crowded room. Vicki was nowhere to be seen. The L's were playing their hit song, "The King of Polyester." With all her heart, Sierra wished she could slip back into the happy crowd and forget what had just happened with Amy. But there was no way. She couldn't spot Vicki, and she had no money. Her only choice was to drive home. Either that or hang out with the other penniless fans who hovered around the door, eagerly snatching the scraps of music that the cranked-up speakers randomly flung in their direction.

"This is pathetic," Sierra muttered to herself. She considered going around to the backstage door and trying to convince someone there that she was with the band. Randy would vouch for her and get her back inside. And then what? How could she relax and have a good time knowing what a jerk she had just made of herself with Amy and Nathan?

Dejected, Sierra drove home and comforted herself by deciding she could spend the rest of the evening working on Paul's Christmas present. That's what she probably should have planned to do all along.

She couldn't decide if she would tell Paul what had happened tonight. Lately she had been writing everything that happened to her. But all she had heard from him was the poetic letter right before Thanksgiving and then that quick note earlier in the week when he told her his birthday was on the tenth. Even though she had written to him daily, giving him every detail of her life, he hadn't responded as often or with as much detail.

Still, there was always tomorrow's mail. Sierra told

herself that often. Weekends seemed long since no mail came on Sundays. Yet every Monday she would check the mailbox with as much hope as she had felt on Saturday. If no letter from Paul appeared, she stored up that hope and kept it ready to pull out again on Tuesday.

Sierra parked her car in front of the house and glanced at the gas gauge. The arrow teetered on the red zone. She knew the next time she started up the car it had better be to drive straight to a gas station. But how much gas could she buy with 37 cents?

The way Sierra felt at the moment, all she wanted to do was hide in her room, put on some sad music, and work on Paul's gift. She walked in the front door, intending to do just that.

Her father called to her from the living room. Her parents were sitting on the couch, watching a movie with Gavin and Dillon.

"You're home earlier than we expected," her mom said.

Deciding to skip the reasons for her early arrival, Sierra said, "Yes, well, it was fun, but I have stuff to do."

"Mind if we have a talk first?" her dad said.

Sierra did mind. She knew this would be the talk about her going to school in Scotland.

"It's a nice night," her dad said. "Why don't we go out on the porch swing?"

"I'll make some coffee," her mom said.

Sierra's heart sank. When her mother made coffee and brought it to her father on the porch swing, it meant a long talk. Some of the talks they had had on the front porch had been wonderful and sweet, such as the night she returned from her trip to England. Tonight Sierra imagined it would be a painful conversation in which she would have to defend herself and try to prove she was mature enough to make her own decisions. The week had been so busy that she hadn't done any of the research she had offered to do on the university or the loans. She didn't have any fuel to feed her fired-up desire to go to Edinburgh. The conversation could only go in favor of her dad at this point. And she had a pretty good idea he hadn't changed his opinion on the subject.

She followed her dad out to the porch, grabbing a throw blanket off the couch on the way. The night was clear, which meant it was cooler than when the clouds hovered low like a down comforter over the city, turning the sky a dull cream color.

"I thought we should talk about you and Paul," her dad began.

"Why?" Sierra heard herself say. She quickly added, "I mean, I thought the issue was about my going to school in Scotland, not about Paul."

"The two seem to be connected," her dad said. His voice was calm and welcoming.

Sierra knew she could talk to her father about anything. She always had been able to. However, now she felt she should distance herself from him to prove she was old enough and wise enough to make her own decisions. She was reluctant to let down her defenses.

"Tell me about your relationship with Paul," her dad said. "You mentioned the other day you've been writing to each other."

Sierra nodded, not volunteering any information.

"How often do you write to him?"

"Pretty often," Sierra said.

"Every day? Every week? Twice a day?"

"I don't know. About every day."

"And how often does he write to you?"

"About every day," Sierra said.

Her dad raised an eyebrow. "When did you last receive a letter from him?"

"A few days ago."

"And it was a long, detailed letter?"

"No, it was short. But the one before that was really long."

"When did that one come?"

"The Wednesday before Thanksgiving."

"What about before that letter?"

"I guess that was the package with his picture."

"Was there a letter with that package?"

"No." Sierra was beginning to do the math in her own head. A full week and a half had passed between the picture and the letter that followed it.

Mr. Jensen paused and was about to say something when Sierra said, "I guess he writes to me more like every week or every week and a half."

Her dad nodded.

"It just seems as though it's more often. I know he's thinking of me more than that, and I'm certainly thinking of him more than that."

Mrs. Jensen arrived with two mugs of dark, rich coffee and handed one to her husband. Then she sat down in a chair across from the two of them and pulled up the collar on her fleece sweatshirt.

"What kinds of things does Paul say in his letters?" Mr. Jensen said.

"What do you mean?" Sierra felt her defenses rising again.

"I mean, does he say he misses you? That he's looking forward to seeing you again?"

"Well, yes," Sierra said slowly. She couldn't think of an example of when he had actually used those words, but she knew the thought was there. She had certainly said those words to him.

No one spoke for a few moments. The coffee's rich fragrance floated to Sierra's nose.

Funny, Sierra thought. *My parents are right here, and yet we feel miles apart. Why are they questioning me like this? Don't they trust me?*

Across the great distance, she felt they were condemning her for letting herself become emotionally involved with this guy who, as the facts showed, didn't appear to be as emotionally involved with her. It wasn't that way, though. Sierra tried to think of a way to make her parents understand.

Paul writes me poems. Sierra stopped mid-thought. *Wait a minute! Did he actually write those poems to me? Or did he simply write them and then share them with me? Paul did send me his picture, and he asked for a picture back from me. He wouldn't have done those things if he didn't care about me and want a visual memory of me close to him.*

"I can't believe you guys don't remember what it's like

to be romantically interested in someone and to read between the lines what that other person is saying." Sierra felt her voice quivering. "It seems so unfair that when, for the first time in my life, I'm really, truly, deeply interested in someone, you would try to break it up. Can't you just be happy for me? There is absolutely nothing wrong with Paul and me writing to each other. I don't appreciate you guys trying to make it seem as though I'm doing something wrong."

Sierra stopped. She mentally repeated the last few lines she had said. Something was hauntingly familiar about them. And she knew what it was. Those were the words Amy had spouted when Sierra questioned Amy's relationship with Nathan after their first date.

"I . . ." Sierra paused. "I'm not feeling up to this conversation right now. Would you guys mind if I went to my room and did some thinking? I'd rather talk about all this later."

Mrs. Jensen looked at her husband, and he nodded.

"Okay," Mrs. Jensen said softly.

Sierra started to leave, her head pounding.

"We love you, Sierra," her mother said. "We only want what's best for you. Don't forget that, okay?"

Sierra couldn't think of anything to say. She gave her parents a sad look over her shoulder and disappeared inside the house.

chapter sixteen

"THE THING IS, OUR RELATIONSHIP IS NOTHING like Amy and Nathan's," Sierra said the next day to Randy.

He had shown up at Mama Bear's just as she was going on her lunch break, and he had decided to join her. Usually, Randy spent Saturdays mowing lawns, but the pouring rain today kept him out of the lawn-care business. And the Christmas sales at the mall seemed to have kept holiday shoppers in the stores and out of Mama Bear's.

As a reflection of her goodwill toward everyone this slow Saturday, Mrs. Kraus had offered Randy a free cinnamon roll, frosted and warmed the way he liked it. She suggested that Randy and Sierra sit at one of the corner tables and enjoy the afternoon lull.

Sierra pushed her empty carton of milk away and leaned closer to confide in Randy. "I mean, with Amy and Nathan it was physical right from the start. With Paul, it's a spiritual connection. We enjoy each other's company emotionally. I guess you could say we're kindred spirits."

Randy listened, offering no comment, judgment, or agreement.

Sierra continued. "I just don't understand why my parents are making such an issue out of this. I'm totally pure. They know that. You know that. Everyone knows that! If they are so convinced I'm blowing it, then what is the point of having this?" She stuck out her right hand to Randy, drawing attention to the gold band on her ring finger. It was the purity ring her dad had given her. "Answer me that? What good is it for my parents to say they trust me, or they're proud of my choices, if they can't understand why this relationship with Paul is so wonderful? Why would they want to ruin it for me?"

Randy didn't answer. He just slowly raised an eyebrow and reached for the cinnamon roll in front of him.

"What?" Sierra challenged.

Randy stuffed the last bite of roll into his mouth.

"You did that so you wouldn't have to answer me, didn't you?"

"No," Randy said, his mouth full. "I don't have a problem talking with my mouth full. I was trying to be polite."

Sierra looked away from the mush in Randy's mouth. He swallowed and smacked his lips loudly.

"Just answer me this," she said, turning back to her buddy. "Why would my parents act as if something were wrong with my relationship with Paul?"

"Is there?" Randy asked.

"Is there what?"

"Something wrong with it?"

"No! Everything is great. It's better than great. It's fantastic."

Randy didn't respond.

"Am I boring you here?" Sierra gave Randy a careful look. "I seem to be doing all the talking about my problem."

"That's how you solve your problems," Randy said. "You don't need to hear my answers. You always figure it out when you hear yourself talk it through. Remember that night on the backpacking trip when you were trying to figure out how you felt about Drake?"

Sierra remembered all right. It was a humiliating memory. She had poured out her heart to Randy in his dark tent, thinking he was her brother. Then the tent had collapsed on the two of them, announcing to the whole camp that Sierra was where she shouldn't be—in a guy's tent. She wished Randy and she could both forget that night.

"Besides," Randy said, "I don't know what the answer is. I don't even know what the problem is."

Sierra dropped her head in her hands. "Randy, the problem is my parents are hinting I don't have the right perspective on my relationship with Paul." She looked up to make sure Randy was paying attention. "I know they want me to stop writing to him. But why? Is it because they think I'm too young for him? I'm 17! That's old enough to be married in some states."

"It is?" Randy appeared shocked at the thought.

"I think. I don't know. The point is, I'm old enough to know what I want and what's good for me."

"And what's that?"

"Paul!" Sierra stated emphatically. "Haven't you been listening?"

"Of course I have. So tell me. Why is Paul good for you?"

Sierra smiled. "He makes me feel good about myself, and he brings out the creative side of me. I feel warm when I read his letters."

"And he brings you closer to the Lord," Randy added.

"What?"

"Wasn't that one of your criteria?" Randy asked. "One time you told me you had written out your standards for dating, and I remember one of your goals was that the guy you're dating would bring you closer to God, and you would do the same for him."

"Oh, right. Yes, of course Paul and I draw each other closer to the Lord." Sierra stated the words as if she were reciting the Pledge of Allegiance.

"Remember when we talked that night in the tent, and you said you were stuck on a steady diet of all your feelings and nothing else?" Randy asked.

Sierra gave him a look of vague recollection.

"I told you not to beat yourself up because you're a sensitive, emotional person," he continued.

She didn't remember.

"I still think you shouldn't beat yourself up because you're a sensitive, emotional person."

"And?"

"And watch your emotional diet."

Sierra leaned back. "That's the best you can do? You're

not going to arm me with statements I can use on my parents?"

Randy shook his head. "The answer will come to you. On your own. Just keep talking about it. It'll become clear what you should do."

Randy's laid-back logic didn't settle with Sierra. What did he mean, watch her emotional diet? The only thing she agreed with was that she usually did figure out solutions to her problems by talking them through.

Her challenge was to figure out whom she going to talk to now that Randy had offered his insights but she was still stuck. Amy? Chances were Amy wasn't talking to Sierra anymore. Neither was Tawni—which was too bad, because on several occasions she had offered Sierra good advice. Plus Tawni would understand what it was like to be emotionally involved with a MacKenzie man, since she was so attached to Jeremy. How about Vicki? Sierra could talk to Vicki, not only about the Paul conflict with her parents, but also about Amy. Sierra decided to call her as soon as work ended.

Glancing at the clock, she realized her break would be over in three minutes. "I have to get back to work," she told Randy. "Thanks for your listening ear."

Randy grinned. "By the way, they paid us $200 for last night."

"Oh, Randy, I forgot to ask. That's great! You guys sounded so good. I was really excited about your big debut—opening for The L's, no less! The place was packed. I think it went perfectly."

"We had some trouble with the third song. You didn't notice?"

"Not at all."

"That's good." Randy appeared pleased. "How come I didn't see you afterward?"

Sierra drew in an exasperated breath. "I kind of got locked out. Vicki had my ticket, and when I went out to check on Amy, I couldn't get back in." She shook her head. "I made such a fool of myself. I saw Amy walking to the parking lot with Nathan, and I thought he was forcing her to go with him, so I . . ."

Randy waited for her to finish.

"I can't believe I did this. I blew an air horn at Nathan and told Amy to run."

Randy's eyes grew wide. He seemed to be trying to stifle a grin. "Did Amy run?"

"No. It turned out they wanted to be together so they could talk. Now they're both furious with me."

"A little is good. A lot . . ."

"I know," Sierra said. "I went overboard again."

Randy slowly grinned. "There are melted marshmallows, and then there are kitchen fires."

"What is that supposed to mean?"

"You know, the Thanksgiving fire at your house. I just thought of it. Melting marshmallows is like a little warmth, and that's good. But too much of a good thing, and your whole kitchen goes up in flames."

Sierra ignored his logic. "What bothers me is that just last week it seemed everything had turned around with Amy. She, Vicki, and I had a great time talking, and the three of us planned to get together every Monday here at Mama Bear's. Now that's all gone up in smoke, to use your analogy."

"Maybe not."

Sierra glanced at the clock again. "My break is over. I'd better get behind the counter. Thanks again for listening to me, Randy."

"Any time." He reached over and gave her wrist a squeeze. "Don't let it get you down. It'll work out—Paul, Amy, the whole thing. It always does. God rules."

"Thanks. I needed your encouragement today. And, hey, congratulations again on how everything went last night."

Just before Randy walked out the door, Sierra said, "Oh, and thanks for giving Vicki a ride home." A hint of curiosity touched her voice.

"Vicki? I didn't give her a ride," Randy said. "Warner did."

"Oh." Sierra turned and made an "uh-oh" face to herself. She couldn't wait to hear Vicki's side of this story.

As it turned out, she didn't get the scoop until Monday afternoon. Saturday night Vicki wasn't home when Sierra called. Then Sierra spent the evening furiously working on Paul's needlework and did the same thing again all Sunday afternoon. That evening the Highland House hot line was busy, and then she stayed up until after midnight to finish her homework. On Monday at lunch, Randy, Warner, and the other guys from the band sat with Vicki and Sierra at lunch, so Sierra couldn't gather any information from Vicki.

The talk around the lunch table and the whole school was about The Beet and whether Randy's group was going to keep the name "Three-Two-One." Randy said it just came to them at the last minute Friday night. Most of the group liked it. The others thought it was lame and promised to come up with something better for them.

After school, Sierra waited by Vicki's locker. When she finally showed up, Sierra said, "Okay, we need to talk. Where do you want to go?"

"To Mama Bear's," Vicki said. "Aren't we supposed to meet Amy there in 15 minutes?"

Sierra leaned her forehead against the locker. "I don't think Amy is speaking to me at the moment."

Vicki looked surprised.

Sierra gave Vicki a sideways glance. "I told you. There's a lot we have to talk about."

"Well, Amy's still talking to me. I think we should go to Mama Bear's as we planned. If there's a problem, we need to talk it through. That's what we all decided last week, isn't it? We missed out on our friendships this past year because none of us worked hard enough at talking things through when we had problems."

Sierra felt a knot in her stomach. She had experienced that same clenching sensation a lot the last few days. Something wasn't right. She was off track, but she couldn't figure out in what way.

Earlier that day, during one of her classes, Sierra pretended to take notes as her teacher lectured, but Sierra had really been writing a letter to Paul, telling him how much she wished he were here so she could talk these things

through with him face-to-face. It had been good to talk to
Randy on Saturday, for the sake of letting off steam. But
Randy didn't have answers. Only vague quips about burning marshmallows and how she shouldn't beat herself up,
since she was a sensitive, emotional person.

With Paul, she knew such a conversation would have
turned out differently. Paul knew her heart. He would hear
her words but still be able to read deeper, between the
lines, the way they did with each other's letters. Paul would
give her the right kind of encouragement and direction.
He would know how she could convince her parents that
her relationship with him was beneficial and how to move
on with Amy.

As it was, Paul wasn't here. That was the down side of
having an absent boyfriend. By the time he received the
letter she wrote him today and answered it, Christmas
would have arrived. By then, anything could have happened.

Suddenly, Sierra remembered what Uncle Mac had said
about love being patient. She had thought she knew what
that meant. Maybe she didn't understand yet. Maybe she
needed to be more patient about Paul's being far away and
more patient with herself and all her goof-ups. And maybe
she needed to be more patient with Amy. She could follow
through on that one right now.

Emerging from her reverie, Sierra adjusted the backpack on her shoulder, looked at Vicki, and said, "Okay,
let's go to Mama Bear's to see if Amy shows up."

"She will," Vicki said confidently. "She needs our little
circle of friendship as much as the two of us do."

chapter seventeen

THE CHEERY BELL OVER MAMA BEAR'S DOOR sounded when Sierra and Vicki stepped into the bakery. The fragrance of gourmet coffee and freshly baked cinnamon rolls rushed to greet them.

"I love the way this place smells," Vicki said. "Do you ever get tired of it when you work here?"

"Not tired of it, but maybe a little immune." Sierra scanned the tables to see if Amy was waiting for them. She wasn't. And they were five minutes late.

"Do you want something?" Vicki asked, heading for the counter. "Some tea? It's my treat."

Sierra appreciated Vicki's generosity. After all, Sierra had borrowed $5 from her dad on Sunday to buy enough gas to drive to the Highland House and to school. Tomorrow was payday, but by the time she paid back everyone she had borrowed money from, little would be left for Christmas presents.

"I'd like some peppermint tea," Sierra said. "Thanks, Vicki." Following Vicki over to the counter, Sierra greeted Mrs. Kraus and then asked her, "Do you remember my friend Amy? Have you seen her in here?"

"I don't think so," Mrs. Kraus said. "It's been kind of busy, though."

She was wearing one of the Christmas aprons she had made for the staff. The red aprons had brown appliquéd teddy bears on the top portion. The teddy bears were wearing headbands with reindeer antlers, and they had red noses. The aprons were cute in a silly way. When Sierra wore hers on Saturday, it drew much more attention than any of Mrs. Kraus's other original apron creations.

"Did I tell you a customer on Saturday asked if she could buy my apron?" Sierra asked.

"No, you didn't. You told her yes, I hope?"

"I told her you made them, and she would have to ask you."

"That's a great idea. I could whip up a couple of extra aprons and hang them around the store. I think I'll do that this evening."

Sierra had a hard time imagining anything that required sewing being whipped up in an evening. Her needlepoint project was taking forever. And it wasn't turning out all that great. The more she worked on it, and the longer she stared at it, the more flaws she saw in it. The joy of the project was long gone.

Mrs. Kraus went to get the hot water for Sierra's tea while Vicki pulled out some money.

"Tell me what happened Friday night," Sierra said. "Randy told me he didn't take you home, but Warner did."

Vicki rolled her eyes and said, "Please, I'm trying to forget."

"I would have called a cab rather than go anywhere alone with Warner."

"We weren't alone," Vicki said. "Four other people were crammed into his car. He dropped me off first. There's really nothing to tell."

"Yes there is. Tell me why Randy didn't give you a ride."

"He already had Tre with him, and when it came time to leave, he didn't offer to squeeze me in."

"But Warner did," Sierra said, taking the small teapot and mug from Mrs. Kraus and thanking her.

"Yep. Good ol' Warner." Vicki smiled at Mrs. Kraus. "And I'd like a mocha latte with cinnamon."

"Our lives don't exactly seem to be working out the way we had planned, are they?" Sierra said.

Vicki paid for their beverages, and the two of them moved over to a table by the front window.

"Oh, I don't know," Vicki said. "I don't have too many complaints at the moment. I don't know why you should either."

"I've been a wreck," Sierra confessed. She slid her chair closer to Vicki so none of the other customers or employees could hear her. "I have this conflict with my parents that's hanging over my head. They're waiting for me to talk it through with them because when they tried to talk to me last Friday, I couldn't discuss it."

"Couldn't discuss what?"

"Paul. They don't like him."

"Excuse me? Would you like to try that one again? Since when did your parents stop liking Paul?"

"Since I started to write him, I guess. They have this

way of making their point without saying it outright, so we kids have to figure out the answer."

"That's better than how my parents handle it. They come right out and tell me everything I'm doing wrong."

"I think I'd rather my parents would do that with this whole Paul issue. I don't know what they have against him. Or against me being involved with him."

"Why don't you ask them?" Vicki suggested. "Your parents would tell you what was wrong if you asked them, wouldn't they?"

"I guess."

"Or is it that you don't want to know what they think?"

"I don't know. I just don't like living with this feeling that something is wrong all the time."

"I know what you mean. I felt that way when my relationship with the Lord was all messed up."

Sierra brushed away the thought that she might have a similar problem. She considered herself a strong Christian. She had been for years. What could be wrong with her relationship with God?

Then an afterthought floated past. How long had it been since she had spent time talking to God or reading her Bible? A long time—weeks. But she had been busy—very busy. Certainly God understood that. It didn't change anything. He still loved her unconditionally, and she was ready to defend her faith on a moment's notice. And she was working on the hot line. People who fall away from God don't volunteer to work on a hot line, do they?

The knot in Sierra's stomach tightened. She had ordered the peppermint tea because she knew it was good for stomachaches. Now she lifted the mug of steaming liquid to her lips and sipped eagerly yet cautiously. She wanted to be soothed, not burned.

The thought stuck with Sierra. That's all she wanted from so many of the things going on in her life. She yearned for a warm, comforting relationship with Paul. She didn't want to get burned or have her heart broken, as Amy had warned. Sierra wanted to have a calm, soothing talk with her parents without getting fired up and burning all the bridges she had built with them over the years. Her "soothe, not burn" thoughts even applied to Amy. She never wanted her actions to burn out of control the way they had Friday night.

"I don't think Amy is going to show up," Sierra said.

Vicki shrugged. "If she doesn't, I'll call her. I think it's important we don't all give up on what started between us last week. If Amy tells me she has a problem with you, you'll agree to talk it through, won't you?"

"Of course," Sierra said. She still felt foolish about what had happened at The Beet. What was it Paul had said to her when they first met? Something about Sierra one day growing into her zeal. Obviously, that hadn't happened yet. She considered herself mature enough to leave home in June and move to Scotland; yet here she was, unable to keep her most important relationships in balance.

"And if you don't mind my saying this, Sierra, I think you should sit down and talk to your parents real soon so you can get this conflict about Paul settled."

"I know," Sierra said. She sipped her peppermint tea and found it brought little comfort.

Amy never showed up, which made Sierra feel even worse. She went home and crawled into bed. When her mother came up to check on her, Sierra said she felt as though she was coming down with something, and she didn't want any dinner. She slept fitfully for about an hour and then sat up, turned on the light, and finished her letter to Paul.

> Is it that I'm too much of a perfectionist? I want everything to be just right. I want my friends to like me, I want my parents not to be mad at me, I want everything to work out and be peaceful. But right now it seems nothing is. Well, some things are okay, I guess. I don't want this letter to be a total downer for you. It's not like there's anything wrong. It's just that a lot of things don't feel completely right. Do you know what I mean?

Sierra stopped writing and sighed. She read the letter, beginning with what she had written in class. The whole letter was nothing but a bunch of words that rambled over the pages and went nowhere. Sierra crumpled it up and tossed the paper ball toward her trash can. That wasn't the kind of letter she wanted Paul to read on the train. Her crazy string of pathetic words was not what he needed for encouragement. Since that's what his letters brought her, Sierra knew her letters should bring him the same thing. She refused to let herself write to him when she was so distraught.

A tear pushed its way to the corner of Sierra's eye. "I can't do anything right," she accused herself. "What's wrong with me? I can't even write to Paul anymore. And my relationship with Paul is the most important thing in my life."

Hearing herself state her feelings aloud shocked Sierra. She repeated her words to make sure she had heard them correctly.

"Paul is the most important thing in my life."

That was a sobering revelation. Had Paul taken the place in her heart where God had always been? Years ago she had decided her relationship with Christ was the most important one and always would be. Sometimes, when she informed others that such was the case, her words carried a bragging tone, but she had confessed that and gone on. Her bragging hadn't changed God's place in the very center of the garden of her heart.

Now when she closed her eyes and tried to imagine her heart's garden, she couldn't see the Lord anywhere. Instead, she saw images of Paul. And it wasn't that Paul had forced himself into that place in her heart. She had put him there. She had also slowly but surely started to ignore God and had stopped spending time with Him. The hollow aching in her stomach began to make sense.

"Sierra?" Her mom called to her from the other side of the closed bedroom door and knocked softly. The door opened, and Mrs. Jensen stepped in, holding the remote phone in her hand. "It's Tawni. She wants to talk to you."

chapter eighteen

"ELLO?" SIERRA ADJUSTED HERSELF ON THE BED
as her mother handed her the phone and left
the room.

"Hi. Mom says you're not feeling well." Tawni's voice
sounded sympathetic.

"I'm okay."

"I hope you don't have the flu. It's been going around
here. They say it's pretty bad this year."

"I think I'll be okay." Sierra plunged in before Tawni
had a chance to say any more. "Tawni, I still feel bad about
saying the thing about Reno at the restaurant. I know it
bothered you a lot. I'm sorry."

"It did bother me," Tawni said. "It bothered me more
than it should have. I'm sorry, too."

Sierra felt that at least with this relationship she could
begin to breathe a little easier. Maybe she should open up
to Tawni and tell her about the revelation regarding how
Sierra had made Paul too much the center of all her
thoughts, feelings, and hopes.

But before Sierra could start, Tawni said, "I wanted to

tell you what happened today because I know you've been praying for me."

Sierra looked down. She couldn't tell her sister that she hadn't prayed for anyone or anything for many weeks.

"I received a phone call from Lina. Lina Rasmussen. My birth mother."

Sierra sat up straight, eager to hear all the details.

"She's a Christian, Sierra. She was so excited when she heard I was a Christian, too. And she's coming here in two weeks so we can meet."

"Oh, Tawni, that's amazing! And exactly what you've been wanting for so long."

"I know! I can't believe it all happened so fast. I was just telling Mom and Dad that she said my letter was shuffled to the bottom of her desk, and she opened it last Friday. She spent the whole weekend praying about how to respond, and then she called me. I just answered the phone, and there she was. It was a huge shock."

"For both of you, I'm sure. What does she sound like?"

"She sounds sweet, but with a little bit of an edge to her voice, if you know what I mean."

Sierra smiled to herself. She knew exactly what her sister meant, since that's the way Tawni came across.

"I told her I was modeling, and Lina said she modeled professionally for three years before she went back to school. Isn't that amazing?"

"Wow! This whole thing is amazing. You're going to love having a face to put with her voice now, aren't you? I mean, you found out her name and where she lived, then what she sounds like, and now you're going to get to see her face. I can't even imagine how excited you must be."

"Thanks, Sierra. I knew you would understand. You guys are the first ones I've told. As soon as I hung up with Lina, I called Mom and Dad. They're happy for me, I know, but they had all kinds of cautions and advice for me. I needed someone to be completely happy for me."

"I'm very happy for you," Sierra said. "This is a huge thing in your life."

"Thank you." Tawni sniffed quietly, apparently unable to speak for a moment.

Sierra filled in the silence by asking, "Do you still think you'll go to UNR in January? I mean, did you really want to take classes there, or was it like Wesley and the others suggested, that you were eager to meet Lina?"

Tawni sniffed again. "I don't know. A little of both, I suppose. I can't explain how important it is for me to see her. No one seemed to understand that. They all thought I was being psychotic to go there, knowing I'd be around her. But if she wasn't going to answer my letter, how else was I going to get what I needed? At least that was my thinking at the time. I know it wasn't real healthy. Everything has changed now that she's called."

"I'm sure she wants to see you as badly as you want to see her."

"I hope so."

"It's obvious she does," Sierra said. "Otherwise she wouldn't have called and made the plans."

"I hope you're right."

"I'll be honest. I haven't been right about a lot of stuff lately. But I think I'm right about this."

"Problems?" Tawni asked, inviting Sierra to open up.

She hesitated and then decided Tawni would be a good person to give Sierra her perspective.

"How can you tell if you're obsessed with something or someone?"

Tawni paused, then said defensively, "Are you trying to say you think I've been obsessed with finding my birth mother?"

"No, no. I'm saying . . . well, okay, I'll just come out and tell you. I'm asking about Paul. How do I know if I'm imagining the relationship is more than it is? And how do I know if I've weakened my commitment to the Lord by becoming too wrapped up in Paul?"

"If you're asking, then it means you've probably gone overboard."

"Great," Sierra muttered.

"Otherwise you wouldn't be feeling that there's a problem. It's the old theory of 'When in doubt, don't.' "

"How do you have a good relationship, then? I mean, if you really, really, really care about the other person, how do you not become wrapped up in him?"

"I've always been of the opinion that you shouldn't change what's important to you when you enter into a close relationship. You keep doing the things that make you strong and healthy, and then you have more to offer the other person. Otherwise, you slowly start to lose your life and your identity and become unbalanced trying to please the other person."

Sierra thought about Amy's saying she had given up all

her friends and other interests when she began going out with Nathan.

"For instance," Tawni said, "I started to attend a Bible study on Thursday nights when I moved here. It's for college-age women, and I need it to keep me on track with the Lord. When I started to date Jeremy seriously, he kept asking me out on Thursday nights because he had that night open. It was one of the only nights he didn't have to work or go to class. But I kept my commitment to the Bible study because that time makes me stronger and provides me with more to offer in my relationship with Jeremy. Does that make sense?"

"Sort of. But Paul's not here. It's not the same thing."

"Yes it is. Have you given up other important things in your life to spend time writing to Paul?"

Sierra knew the answer was yes. She just didn't want to admit to her sister that the main chunk of time she had given up was her time with the Lord. It was especially painful to realize that it had been the first thing to go. She still found time to shop, watch TV, and talk on the phone. But she never seemed to have any time left in her day to read her Bible.

Tawni continued before Sierra had to confess. "I guess what seems to be working so well with Jeremy and me is that both of us have other friends, activities, and commitments, and we stay involved with all of them. Then, when we get together, which is about once or twice a week, we have all kinds of stuff to talk about. We don't talk to each other every day. Have you been trying to write to Paul every day?"

"Not *every* day," Sierra said.

"Maybe you need to pull back and just give yourself one night a week that you spend a couple of hours writing to him. That's how it would be if you were dating. Or at least that's how it is with Jeremy and me."

Sierra knew her sister was probably right. Between the gifts she had worked on for Paul, the letter writing, and the daydreaming, not a day had gone by during the past few months that Sierra hadn't dedicated several hours to Paul.

"I know you're right," Sierra said to Tawni. "I'm just beginning to realize some pretty important facts about relationships. One is that I need to pull back and not write Paul so often."

"How often does he write you?"

"That's what's funny. I was sure he was writing to me every day. I really believed that. Then Dad started to quiz me, and I realized Paul writes only about once every week or once every two weeks. And his letters are never as long and detailed as mine are."

"That's a good measuring point for you," Tawni said. "It will be better if you respond to him at the same level that he's pursuing you. Believe me, I've seen far too many of my friends become lopsided in a new dating relationship and pretty soon the teeter-totter gets too heavy on their side. All of a sudden, Plop! There they are, crashed in the dirt and devastated because they had thought everything was going so well."

"I don't want this relationship to crash in the dirt," Sierra said quietly.

"I know exactly what you mean," Tawni said. "I can tell you from experience that the best way to nurture a relationship with a MacKenzie man is with patience."

"So I've heard," Sierra murmured. Sierra knew she could do that. She could be patient. She could pull back and respond to Paul at the same level he was communicating with her. And she could definitely invest her time in developing other areas of her life.

"Tawni?"

"Yes?"

"Thanks."

A gentle pause enveloped them.

"I needed to hear everything you've told me," Sierra said.

"I should have made more of an effort for us to talk while I was there," Tawni said. "I could tell you were spending a lot of time writing to Paul and thinking about him even when you were with other people."

"I don't think I would have heard your advice. It's like Randy said, I have to talk my problems out, and when I hear myself explaining them, everything begins to make sense and I can accept advice. I know I wouldn't have been ready for advice at Thanksgiving."

"Randy said that, huh? I like Randy. Did he have any other advice for you?"

Sierra started to laugh. "He told me I was like the marshmallows on the sweet potatoes at Thanksgiving. A little fire makes them melt, a lot of fire and the whole kitchen burns down."

Tawni laughed softly. "That's pretty perceptive. What

was that clan motto you showed me for 'MacKenzie' on the stitchery kit you bought?"

Sierra had the needlepoint right beside her, but she didn't need to read the Latin phrase. She had memorized it. "*Lucero non uro*," she repeated.

"Yes, but what did you tell me it meant in English?"

Sierra stopped and stared at the square piece of needlework. She finally understood the key to unlock the great mystery that had kept her stomach in knots. With her heart suddenly open to a new understanding of relationships, she repeated for her sister, " 'I shine, not burn.' "

chapter nineteen

S IERRA WROTE THOSE WORDS—*Lucero non uro*—IN
her journal that night after her phone conversation
with Tawni. According to the last entered date,
Sierra hadn't written out her thoughts and prayers in this
private book for almost two months. Beneath the Latin
words, she wrote a letter to the Lord as freely as she had
been writing letters to Paul for so many weeks. She apologized for ignoring Him and invited Him to again take the
center place in the garden of her heart.

> *I want to shine for You, Lord. I don't want that light
> to burn out. I want to have just the right amount of
> fire—light, warmth, and energy—in my relationship
> with Paul, but I don't want to overdo it and watch the
> whole thing go up in flames.*
>
> *From now on, I want to put You first and keep You
> first. Teach me how to do that, Father. My heart is Yours,
> and all the emotions You made that are stored there. I
> want You to protect my emotions and keep me from
> pouring them out too much at a time. Teach me to be
> patient with myself and with others.*

Sierra continued to write rapidly until her hand started to cramp. It felt so good to get everything out. The only ache she felt in her stomach now was from hunger.

After she finished her prayer-journaling, she went downstairs. It was almost nine, and the house was quiet. She found her dad working on the computer in the study.

"Feeling better?" he asked.

"Much. Pretty exciting news about Tawni."

"Yes, it is. We hope it works out and that she doesn't have unrealistic expectations."

"I think Tawni has realistic expectations of all her relationships. She'll be fine."

Mr. Jensen looked somewhat relieved at hearing Sierra's words. "You know what? You're right. Tawni has always displayed maturity and good insights. She makes wise choices."

Sierra felt like adding, "Not like your other daughter, who manages to make an emotional mess of nearly all of her relationships." But she didn't say that. She remembered Randy's admonition not to beat herself up for being a sensitive, emotional person. That's who she was. That's how she embraced life—with open arms and a vulnerable heart full of feelings. She could see how Tawni's self-discipline and sparing use of emotions had helped her to make wise choices over the years. Still, Sierra would rather be a bubbly bumbler than an aloof thinker like Tawni.

"If you and Mom have some time tomorrow, I think I'll be ready for our talk."

"Good," her dad said. "We'll talk after dinner. By the way, three e-mails are here for you."

"Really? Who are they from?"

"One from your friend in Switzerland, and two from someone named Katie. Would you like me to print them out?"

"Yes. Thanks."

Sierra realized it had been weeks since she had written to either Christy or Katie. Those were two other friendships she didn't want to lose, but she sure hadn't made an effort to maintain them while she was going overboard with Paul. Sierra thought of the items she had bought at the gift shop that she had intended to use to create a tea party for herself. Since her funds were low for Christmas, she decided she would send the tea party to Christy just as she had sent the instant birthday party to Paul. She would have to think of something else creative to send to Katie.

Gathering the e-mail messages from the printer, Sierra went into the kitchen to fix her favorite snack. She called it "mush." It was a mug of smashed-up graham crackers mixed with just enough milk to make them wet and soft. For flair, Sierra added a handful of miniature marshmallows. Then she sat at the kitchen counter to enjoy her creation and to read her messages.

Christy's was short. She said she was learning a lot at the orphanage in Basel and that she and Todd had been keeping in touch through letters. Sierra remembered how concerned Christy had been that her relationship with Todd would suffer when she went to Switzerland for a year, since, in all the years she had known him, he had never written to her. Well, Sierra vaguely recalled something about a coconut Todd had sent Christy, but that couldn't have held much of a message. Sierra smiled to think that Todd was now writing letters to Christy.

Sierra also thought about how powerful letters could be. Maybe that's why she had become involved with Paul so quickly. They both seemed to say in their letters what they probably would never say face-to-face.

She decided she wanted to reread all of Paul's letters with her new, clearer understanding of what their relationship should be about. She carried the e-mails and the little bit of mush left in the mug upstairs and went to the antique dresser in her bedroom. In the top drawer, she had placed all of Paul's letters, which were tied together with a ribbon. Flopping onto her bed, she untied the ribbon and read each letter in order. There were only eight letters and two postcards. She knew he had received at least twice that many from her. It made her wonder if he had saved her letters or tossed them once he had written back.

What surprised Sierra most as she read Paul's words with a less-expectant heart was that, though his letters were warm and personal, nothing in them indicated he was falling in love with her, as she had supposed. Clearly, he cared about her and was interested in her as a person, but nothing hinted at his being as emotionally wrapped up in her as she had become in him. Painful as that realization was, it was freeing, too. The truth was setting her free. She could continue to write to him, care about him, and even daydream a little.

Sierra turned over onto her back and stared at the ceiling. She had no way to judge the tone of the letters she had sent Paul. Had she smeared her emotions all over the pages in a fashion as messy as she had been processing her feelings? No, some of the letters, she knew, were calm. Some were newsy. Some were dotted with teasing and joking in response to experiences Paul had written about.

Again, Sierra remembered Randy's advice not to beat herself up. She couldn't change the past. Maybe she had gone too far emotionally with this relationship. But now she knew that she could start over. She could trust God for this area of her life and be more responsible in how much of her emotional self she gave away. She had all kinds of hope for a fresh start.

As it turned out, Sierra didn't have an opportunity to talk to her parents on Tuesday. The chance for the three of them to sit down didn't materialize until Sunday afternoon. That additional time allowed Sierra to work through a lot for herself.

One night she reviewed her written goals for dating and her purity creed. She had some amendments to add now that she realized that saving herself for her future husband included saving herself emotionally as well as physically.

When Sierra and her parents finally sat down together in the living room Sunday afternoon, she brought her lists with her.

"I guess you both know I've kind of been going through a lot lately, and I guess the easiest way to explain things is to say God has been teaching me a bunch of important lessons. First let me say I'm sorry I've pulled away from you guys and claimed I was old enough to make my own decisions. I realize now I do best when I take advice and input from other people. I should have listened to what you were trying to say about Paul rather than being defensive."

"What was it you heard us trying to say about Paul?" her dad asked.

"I think you wanted me to see that I was getting too involved emotionally and that maybe the feeling wasn't mutual."

Her parents both nodded.

Sierra pulled out all her papers. She felt like a junior lawyer presenting her case. First she showed her parents two of Paul's letters, which was something she hadn't done before.

"You can see that he's interested in corresponding with me, which is what I felt I had to prove to you. But I also see more clearly now that he's not approaching our friendship on the same emotional level I've been operating on."

Sierra then handed her parents her revised list of dating goals and her purity creed. "The biggest thing I've learned is that purity and waiting in a relationship don't pertain only to the physical. The feeling happens first in the heart, I think. When I become emotionally involved, I'm giving away a part of my heart, just as physical involvement is giving away your body."

She felt a little embarrassed admitting these thoughts to her parents. Yet she knew it was the only way to make clear what God had been teaching her.

"I think I'm beginning to understand that the area of emotions might be a challenge for me, whereas the physical side, well, that's nonexistent. But I see now that I'm a pretty emotional person, and I seem to get way more into my feelings than other people do."

"That's part of your personality," her mom said. "Even when you were a little girl, you were more emotional than the other five kids. Don't be ashamed of that. God gave you that level of sensitivity as a gift."

Sierra nodded. She really felt as if she were beginning to understand that. "But like any other gift, I can misuse it, can't I?"

Her dad nodded quickly several times.

"So, being the free spirit that I am, I have to be more on my guard than Tawni or Wesley, because they approach relationships with more logic than feelings."

"That's a wise insight, Sierra." Her dad looked over the papers she placed in front of him. "But don't sell yourself short in the logic department. This is very well thought out. It shows maturity."

"Does it also show you that I have a better understanding of what's going on in my relationship with Paul and that I'm ready to continue the relationship at a lower level of intensity?"

"Yes," her mom said.

"Definitely," her dad said. "We trust you to take it from here. Thanks for being so open."

"Thanks for being so understanding."

Sierra picked up her pages and felt a sweet calm coming over her. This is how communication usually was between her and her parents, and this is how she wanted it to always be.

She returned her letters and other papers to her room

and spent about 20 minutes halfheartedly picking up the endless clutter on her floor. She had homework to do and Christy's Christmas tea-party present to wrap and mail, and in an hour and a half she was supposed to report to the Highland House for her Sunday shift on the hot line. Tonight was going to be her last night until after Christmas vacation, so she didn't feel right about canceling on Uncle Mac.

Sierra made herself sit down and do her homework. When it came time to leave for the Highland House, she tucked her picture of Paul in her backpack. Last week she had mentioned it to Uncle Mac, and he had asked her to bring it so he could see it.

chapter twenty

THE EVENING SKY HUNG LOW AS SIERRA DROVE TO the Highland House. The dull gray hinted at rain, so Sierra had pulled on her black, rolled-brim hat. She had also stuck the needlework in her backpack, with the hope that she still might finish it before Christmas. Sierra had already decided that if she didn't, she would send Paul a homemade card rather than frantically try to find something else to buy him. The card would wish him well and promise that a little something would be in the mail soon. He would have to be patient.

Uncle Mac stood by the back entrance, holding open the door for Sierra as she arrived.

"Hi, how's it been going tonight?" Sierra asked, stepping into the warm room.

"Good. It's been real slow. I have you set up over here, on this phone tonight."

Uncle Mac led Sierra to a corner where a phone sat on a round, wooden table. He had been trying to fix up the phone areas to make them more private so that the counselors wouldn't feel distracted while they talked to callers.

It was a challenge because the room wasn't very large, but it was clean and well lit.

"Here's the picture of Paul I told you about," Sierra said, laying her backpack on the table and unzipping the front pouch.

Uncle Mac took the picture and looked long and hard at his nephew. "How's he doing? Have you heard from him?"

"I received a letter right after Thanksgiving, but it was only half a page. I think he's still enjoying school, but he says his grandmother rations the heat in her house, and it's been cold."

Uncle Mac laughed. "That sounds like my mother. She has a heart of gold, but trust me, nothing is ever wasted when she's around. Everything is measured to the minute." Uncle Mac placed Paul's picture on the round table. It made the desk look as if it were Sierra's personal area.

"You know it's already Monday morning in Edinburgh," he said.

Sierra waited for Uncle Mac to make his point.

But all he said was, "You prefer tea, don't you?"

Sierra nodded, not following his logic.

"I'll be right back." He went out the side door that led to the kitchen of the homeless shelter. Sierra could hear the other hot-line volunteer as he spoke on the phone at a table across the room. She recognized the points he was going through with the caller; they were from the blue section in the counseling notebook.

All the counseling topics were listed on the side tabs. In the weeks that she had been helping out, Sierra had grown more confident and had to refer only one of the calls to Uncle Mac because she didn't feel she could handle it. The rest were pretty much "by the book."

The front door opened, and Sierra looked up. Amy walked in with Vicki beside her.

"Hi," Vicki said cheerfully. "Will we get you in trouble if we talk to you?"

"I don't think so," Sierra said slowly. "I'll have to answer the phone if someone calls."

"That's okay," Vicki said.

"So, what's up?" Sierra asked.

"We went by your house." Vicki pulled up a chair and sat across from Sierra. Amy did the same. "Your parents said they thought it would be okay if we came by and bugged you."

Amy and Sierra still hadn't made eye contact. Sierra turned to Amy, determined to look at her until Amy looked back.

"Amy, I'd like to apologize about the air horn last week. I still can't believe I did that. I'm sorry."

Amy met Sierra's gaze. "It's okay. You thought you were helping me."

"I'm learning that sometimes I lunge ahead because of my feelings instead of thinking things through."

"We all do that," Amy said.

"Oh, not me," chimed in Vicki. "I'm completely calm . . . unless Randy happens to be around. Now, if only he would notice when *I'm* around."

The girls laughed.

Then, with a sigh Sierra said, "It always seems to come

back to patience, doesn't it? Uncle Mac tried to remind me of that a few weeks ago. You know, from 1 Corinthians 13: 'Love is patient.'"

Vicki and Amy both looked at Sierra, waiting for her to explain herself.

"I've realized," Sierra said, lowering her voice, "I need to take a few steps back in my feelings for Paul. I need to be patient."

"I guess it's my turn for a true confession," Amy said. "Nathan and I didn't get back together. But we did talk things through, and I think that was good for both of us. I just want to move on from here." Amy motioned to the sign above the bulletin board and read it aloud, " 'A safe place for a fresh start.' That's what I want."

"Good," Vicki said, leaning forward and reaching for Paul's picture. "I'm all for moving on. Especially with the three of us. Everyone friends again?"

Sierra nodded. Amy nodded.

"This is such a good picture," Vicki said, examining Paul more closely. "Patient or not, he's going to love the picture of you in your green dress."

"Didn't I tell you? The pictures didn't come out. I ended up sending him one my mom snapped of me right after I gave the dog some water."

"Sounds glamorous," Vicki said with a laugh.

"I can't believe I didn't tell you. The guy at the one-hour photo place actually bought a copy to put up in their window."

"What did you look like?" Amy asked, taking the picture of Paul from Vicki and looking at it.

Sierra gazed down at her fisherman's knit sweater and tilted her hat-topped head at her friends. "Just like this. I looked like me."

Uncle Mac came in with a mug of tea for Sierra. "Looks like I didn't make enough. Tea sound good to both of you ladies?"

"Sure. Thanks," Vicki answered for them.

Uncle Mac slipped back out, and the phone next to Sierra rang, causing her to jump. She reached for it on the second ring. Vicki and Amy motioned that they would be quiet.

"Highland House Teen Hot Line, Sierra speaking."

After a fraction of a second delay, the male voice on the other end said, "Oh, is it now? I thought I was talking to the Daffodil Queen."

Sierra felt as though her heart had stopped. Both her friends noticed the sudden change in her expression and leaned forward.

When her voice finally found it's way out of her mouth, Sierra whispered, "Paul?"

Vicki's and Amy's mouths dropped open.

"All I can afford is a three-minute call, so I'll talk fast. Thanks for your gift. I have your picture here in front of me. It looks just like you, Sierra."

"Th-that's funny," she stammered. "I have your picture right here, too. I brought it to show Uncle Mac." Sierra reached for the frame and looked into Paul's face as she listened to his words.

"And the party food you sent is going to be eaten

tonight with great enjoyment. Very creative of you. Thanks."

"You're welcome. I'm glad you like it. I hope you have a happy birthday."

"Thanks. I think I will. Tell Uncle Mac hi for me."

"I will," Sierra said. "He just stepped out, but we were talking about you only a few minutes ago. Were your ears burning?"

Paul laughed. He sounded happy—content, yet slightly amused. "It's not quite dawn here at my grandmother's cottage, and believe me, nothing around here is burning."

Sierra laughed. "She's still rationing the heat, I take it."

"Let me just say I'm looking forward to my dash to the early train. It will make me warmer than I've been all weekend."

Sierra smiled but didn't fill the moment of silence with any words.

"Look," Paul continued, "my three minutes are about up, but I want to be sure to say what I called for. I want to ask a favor of you."

"Sure," Sierra said.

"Could you pray for me this week? I have exams, and I'm trying to make some decisions about the future. You're my prayer warrior, Sierra. Will you pray?"

"Of course," Sierra said.

"Great!" Paul sounded relieved. "I have to run. Thanks, Sierra. I'll write to you after exams. Bye."

With that, the line went dead.

Sierra felt a pinch in her heart. *You're my prayer warrior* echoed in her head. Paul hadn't said, "You're my long-distance girlfriend," "my kindred spirit," "my heart friend," or any of the descriptions she would have imagined even a few days ago. She was now, as she had been from the very beginning, Paul's prayer warrior.

And that was a good thing. That hadn't changed while she had been on her emotional spree, vividly imagining what she and Paul meant to each other. She realized now she hadn't had much time to pray for him while she was busy daydreaming about him.

"Sierra?" Vicki said cautiously, waving her hand in front of Sierra's dazed face. The phone, which Sierra still held in her hand, was emitting a sharp dial tone. "Was that really Paul? From Scotland?"

Sierra blinked. She hung up the phone and nodded.

"What did he say?" Amy asked, leaning forward.

"He received my picture. I think he liked it."

"That's good," Vicki said. "What else?"

"He asked me to pray for him."

Amy leaned back, looking disappointed in Sierra's report.

"He called me his prayer warrior."

At that moment something wonderful happened in Sierra's heart. She felt calm and warm. The wild emotional surges she had been experiencing quieted within her. Her prayers for Paul, offered from a clean heart, could cut through the thick fog of all her feelings and reach the very throne of God. And God answers prayers. She knew that to be true.

"Was that all?" Vicki asked. "Didn't he say anything else?"

"No," Sierra said, leaning back and enjoying the contentment that had settled on her. "That was all."

Then, with a gleam in her eyes, she smiled at Paul's photo and added, "And for now, that's enough."

Don't Miss These Captivating Stories in
THE SIERRA JENSEN SERIES

THE CHRISTY MILLER SERIES

If you've enjoyed reading about Sierra Jensen, you'll love reading about Sierra's friend Christy Miller.

9803

FOCUS ON THE FAMILY®

LIKE THIS BOOK?

Then you'll love *Brio* magazine! Written especially for teen girls, it's packed each month with 32 pages on everything from fiction and faith to fashion, food . . . even guys! Best of all, it's all from a Christian perspective! But don't just take our word for it. Instead, see for yourself by requesting a complimentary copy.

Simply write Focus on the Family, Colorado Springs, CO 80995 (in Canada, write P.O. Box 9800, Stn. Terminal, Vancouver, B.C. V6B 4G3) and mention that you saw this offer in the back of this book. You may also call 1-800-232-6459 (in Canada, call 1-800-661-9800).

You may also visit our Web site (www.family.org) to learn more about the ministry or find out if there is a Focus on the Family office in your country.

— — —

Chances are you'll like the "Nikki Sheridan" books, too! Based on a high-school junior named Nikki, whose life is turned upside down after one night's mistake, it's a series that deals with real issues teens today face.

Have you heard about our "Classic Collection"? It's packed with drama and outstanding stories like Louisa May Alcott's *Little Women*, which features the complete text—updated for easier reading—and fascinating facts about the author. Did you know that the Alcott's home was a stop on the Underground Railroad? It's true! And every "Classic" edition packs similar information.

Call Focus on the Family at the number above, or check out your local Christian bookstore.

Focus on the Family is an organization that is dedicated to helping you and your family establish lasting, loving relationships with each other and the Lord. It's why we exist! If we can assist you or your family in any way, please feel free to contact us. We'd love to hear from you!